Galata

Also by Ben Gribbin from Elsewhen Press

THOMAS SILENT
or, *Why there are no more mermaids*

Galata

Ben Gribbin

Elsewhen Press

Galata
First published in Great Britain by Elsewhen Press, 2023
An imprint of Alnpete Limited

Elsewhen Press, PO Box 757, Dartford, Kent DA2 7TQ
www.elsewhen.press

British Library Cataloguing in Publication Data.
A catalogue record for this book is available from the British Library.

ISBN 978-1-915304-29-2 Print edition
ISBN 978-1-915304-39-1 eBook edition

Designed and formatted by Elsewhen Press

To Eleanor Gribbin
light of my life and my own dearest wife

Chapter One

Sometimes, in mid February, it snows in Galata. It is a temperate city with a lot of rain, except for the summer. The seasons come later here, deceptively late. The summer comes when you have almost given up on it, in a brief shudder of dryness in late August. The winter too comes late, if you call snow winter, and half of the years doesn't come at all. When it does come, it is a beautiful but a risky business. You can never quite be sure where the flooding is. A thin layer of water, even salt water, can freeze in such cold. And when it freezes, snow covers it. You only discover *that* when the ice beneath the snow cracks and your shoes are suddenly filled with water so near freezing it seems to have gone beyond it.

In some ways, the people of the city are grateful for the snow when it comes because it is the only time they can convince themselves that their city is not dying. They hold markets, taking care to place the stalls only on the dry land, and they look out on the frozen water of the lower squares and pretend that the thin level of snow covering it is true land; that the cobbles below are not, in fact, haunted by salt water. The illusion only ever lasts a few hours, on the occasional morning. Then the tide retreats a little, the ice cracks under pressure, the snow falls through the fissures and the city is shown for what it is again.

The people here are devoted to two different things, or two sides of the same. One is forgetting; blocking away the knowledge that their city is slowly sinking into the sea. The other is remembering; looking up at the stone angels and the high churches and the faded engravings of the dead. Trying to ignore the saltwater damage to metal signs. The festival that is coming should do both. Forgetting, and remembering. The festival should assuredly do both.

Every place has a moment when it is regarded as being born. For anywhere old, that is generally the moment when it was first recorded; the first record that still remains. For Galata that comes exactly one thousand years ago. It is a brief mention in a taxation document, and records nothing more than the cattle kept in the fields behind a small seaside village, and the estimated population. It gives no idea about the place as it truly is or was. If you are looking for that, you must look forward over four hundred years to the *Reflections* of Saint Mattheus, a traveller from Rome. Read what he says about the place he visited in 1464:

"And we walked across the forest to the valley, to the floating city. Here they cast petals on the water in spring. The houses are built of wood and on wooden slats. The roads are rivers and thin boats float between the houses. The sun sets on the waters out to sea, and rises behind the city, between the hills. The people are dark haired and choleric. We did not dare stay the night amongst them, although they declare themselves Christian. There was illness amidst the beauty, and much of the Lord's work still to be done."

Obviously by the fifteenth century Galata was a place to be reckoned with, a city. It benefited from being mentioned by the famous *Reflections*. People are attracted by beauty blended with sickness, and this city has far more than its share of dead poets.

In some ways you could say that the extract above marks the true start for the place. It encouraged the Manvilles to move in, choosing the colder beauty of this northerly city over the dry security of more southern lands. That ancient family brought money in abundance, and money attracts architects and artists and the poets, dead or otherwise. All of the greatest architecture of the place, the high gothic towers and the later neo-classical domes, date from after St Mattheus' visit. As he notes, there was much of the Lord's work still to be done, and the city set about this work in earnest.

While this visit has been said for many years to mark the true start of the city, all of that is to be forgotten soon, at least for a week. For the coming year marks the thousandth anniversary of that first mention of Galata as a clumsy village wrestling with the water. Every year, New Year's Day is recognised with the crowning of the year's Queen. But every hundred years, rather than a day of celebration, a week is been put aside. The seas are rising quickly now, with global warming cracking the ice-caps far away. The waters slosh around the market-place at high tide, and a full moon is something to fear, dragging the ocean upward with its distant, pulling strength. The thousand year anniversary must be marked. There will not be many more anniversaries of note, before this city sinks into the sea. It will not last another century, not unless words stop water.

Winter snow comes late here. But the rains that bother the place come early in November, and after that it seems they will never leave. The narrow boats that go up and down the rivers between the houses have cloth spread across them, and the people huddle close for warmth and leap off at the landing docks and race for the dryness of their homes or other people's homes. Normally, December is a bleak month, despite the struggle to celebrate Christmas with fine lines of lights that are strung across the waters. This year it is all different. The atmosphere throughout December has been one of anticipation. Not for Christmas, which comes every year and is generally a disappointment, but for something far more special. The final celebration of the city, the last moments of elation. A great festival that has been planned for twenty years, a wait which has seemed an eternity for the young. The mark of a thousand years of history. A week long celebration, full of all the life this slow-breathing city can still bring together. A last brief time of jubilation, before it all falls down. There was good reason to celebrate New Year's Eve this year. It marked the beginning of something special.

Something that will never come again.

Joseph lives in the suburbs to the east of the central city. This is what will be left of the city when the waters have fully broken through. About a dozen streets on the higher slopes. For a long time it was regarded as poverty to live here. Through the past fifty years, the value of the properties rose slightly as the people became more aware that the ancient, and therefore beautiful parts of the city are crumbling beyond repair. Now, in a last glory or madness, the prices of the area have slumped again. People do not want to buy houses or rooms that will last. They want to be able to say they were the final people to live in the great ancient river-streets of Galata. There is a certain madness in the rich.

Joseph owns a small apartment on a dull street of high houses. These are perhaps eighty years old. Their only virtue is that they have high ceilings, and tall windows. There is also a balcony in every room that faces outward. Today, the first day of the New Year, his head is burning from the memory of too much red wine. Last night he met and kissed Celice, for the first time. They were watching the fireworks when it happened. She'd loved the fact that he was a detective. He hadn't told her how low down he'd been. He hadn't told her that he'd quit; that it sickened him, bored him. That in a way he was glad when his parents died in quick succession, leaving him with the money to support himself.

After the kiss, she had asked him for his phone-number, writing it down on a sheet of notepaper, leaning against a hard bundle of tin foil she had found in her pocket. She had told him she was keeping that for her crown. He had told her she was already a princess, and then they had kissed again.

This morning, his hands are aching and he feels old. Because he feels old now, at thirty-five, he is wondering whether this might be love and struggling to persuade himself that it is. He's retired, partly through choice, and she's almost retired – she's an artist, and to his mind that's the same thing. She would not come home with him. He is glad of that. It is hard for him to convince himself he likes a woman who will come home with him too soon.

Sighing to himself, he looks briefly in the mirror. His forebears would recognise him as one of their own. He is dark-haired and looks close to death, he is so pale and thin. There is a gunshot scar on one arm, red and dull as he stands there in his vest. His youthful skinniness has turned into unhealthiness, although he cannot quite admit that to himself yet. When he is done with the mirror, and with washing his face in water that is a little red with rust, he opens the windows and listens carefully. It is impossible to hear the music this high up and this far away. He only hears cars. Then he dresses simply in old blue jeans and a dark jumper, goes out of the room, and gets into a caged elevator that takes him down to the ground floor.

It is not early but there are still people on these streets, making their way downwards. None of these are dressed in carnival clothes. They are only walking to the centre to watch the parade. The people who are taking part were there hours ago. Every now and then a car will drive past, but this is rare. The people are making their way towards the centre, after all. It is far more sensible to walk. After walking a little way, Joseph turns on to a more main street that has been sealed off from cars. Here there are stalls, selling pamphlets that outline the planned festivities of the week. He takes some money from his pocket, and buys one. He can afford to.

As befits a festival, the celebrations will move towards a climax as the week progresses. This festival is in certain ways almost two celebrations. There are the parades in daylight, for children and wives and people too scared of the dark. These will be filled with gold and green and blue, cheerful music intended to reflect strength. Then there are the celebrations after dark. Fire on the water, or in the sky, or held in blazing torches. In a happy way, though with his head still throbbing, he turns to the first page of the pamphlet and reads what will happen today. There were marches throughout the morning, he sees. At two o'clock this afternoon, the true opening of the festival will take place. The crowning of the Queen of Galata in the marketplace by the cathedral.

Joseph turns the corner of Bereashith street now and knows he is in the true centre of the city. Many hundreds of years ago, when the money came pouring in, this is where it fell. The Manvilles and those among them renamed the streets with Hebrew names, Old Testament names. This is *beginning* street. Further on and further in, there will be Sha-Mayim street and Ha-Mayim street, the street of the waters. All the streets that meet at the marketplace, confusingly, hold the same name. Every one is known as the street of Elohim. There are four of these streets, and in each of them now a parade is taking place. These are not river roads, but they are covered slightly by the tide when the moon is full, as it will be later in the week. For now, the tide stops a little way before them, nearer to the ocean.

Along the main street there are many people, and Joseph sees as he passes a church that the time is now past one o'clock. Really he should eat but he feels too giddy for food. Now he can hear the distant sound of deep drums, more threatening here without the high pitched melodies that carry less far. Here, the people from the parades are beginning to become evident. These are mainly children from the early parade of the morning. They are laughing and fighting in the centre of the streets, excited at the absence of cars. The little girls are all dressed as princesses, with tin foil crowns and blue or green dresses. The boys are also dressed royally, in clumsy cloaks made of curtain cloth, with their best shirts white underneath. All of them made their march in celebration, and all are waiting now to see the real Queen be crowned. A normal girl like them, they have been told. Only seventeen years old, chosen from among the people. All are curious to see who it might be.

Today is the only day in this year's festival that will follow what happens every year. Every New Year's Day, a new Queen is crowned. There is always a lot of ceremony around it that means nothing now. She is always young and, in the language of the ceremony, 'virginal'. She must swear that for a year she will be married only to the city and to God. She is given money, which she gives to her family. For the rest of the year she goes about her business, working in the market or the home, sometimes even studying. There is nothing different about her then, except that she wears throughout the day a circlet of silver that is hundreds of years old. That is the only difference between her and the others, but it is a great one. She symbolises the city throughout the year, and the normality of the rest of her life is just a sign that life will go on.

The streets get wider as Joseph walks, and then grow narrower again as he gets into the old part of the city. Here the houses are built on wooden slats, firm foundations that regularly rot and have to be replaced. It is possible to walk to the main square, but to save time he catches a long boat along one of the canals. People sit in rows of two. He is seated next to a fat woman, middle-aged, with her hair tied in neat knots all across her head. With the cover over the boat and the fat woman sitting between him and the world, Joseph can see next to nothing. He nurses his sore head until they reach one of the dry land streets a little way from the main square. Then all of them get off, tip the boat's driver and make their way into the crowd. Joseph is amused to notice that even the driver is wearing a foil crown, in recognition of the day.

These crowns are everywhere and in very little time Joseph begins to feel out of place. Aware that he will feel ridiculous either wearing a crown or not, he nonetheless bows to the pressure of a trader who has lain perhaps forty identical cheap circlets out on a blanket in the street, all of them woven rapidly but skilfully from tin foil and wire. He pays his money and puts the crown on his head and walks on. The music is growing louder now and very soon he comes upon one of the four processions that meet in the central square. He is in Elohim street, coming in from the north, and the procession is moving slowly. As it moves, one part of it plays music badly, traditional brass melodies undercut by the imperfect beat of drums. The people here are adults, and rather than being dressed royally all are dressed as figures from history. Many of them are already drunk, and many of those who are not are trying to be.

The slowness of the march is annoying but the street is entirely busy with people. In the centre of the road, those who are dressed for the parade are standing proud, wearing false sixteenth century dresses or ridiculous ruffs and dark velvet coats. To their sides and behind, the people who have made no effort now try vaguely to be part of the march, walking slowly with their cheap crowns balanced on damp hair. Eventually they make their way to the square. Every one here is jostling and pressing. Children are being held high on shoulders. They are the only ones who can get a proper view. But the queen, as she is to be, will be visible to anyone when her time comes. In front of the cathedral, a large stand has been set up, of strong oak lattices. After the crowd has waited for a long time, the bishop carefully climbs the ladder that is propped behind this stand. He is an old man now, but still smiles more than you would imagine a bishop would smile. He leans forward on the stand and begins to speak into a microphone. Suddenly his voice is heard from speakers at every corner of the square. It is as though he is everywhere at once. Joseph keeps his eyes on the old man.

"Greatest of cities, city of rivers. We give thanks to Christ the carpenter for the wood on which our city rests, to Christ the fisherman for granting us mastery of the sea. Praise him."

A brief thread of acknowledgement runs through the crowd. The bishop waits for the people to be quiet again, realises they never will and continues.

"One thousand years ago, this city was first recorded. Over those many years, those many lives, so much has changed. We have grown strong, we have grown beautiful. The blind eyes of stone angels overlook our world. They have seen it all. For more than twenty of those years, I have made this speech on New Year's Day and you have stood before me. This year is different. For this is not merely the crowning of our Queen, but the crowning of our city. The mark of one hundred years, the mark of one thousand. A week of celebration, to mark it and to worship it. In a little time, now, our princess will stand here where I stand. She will become the symbol of our city and of our people. Now is a time for celebration.

"They say that our city is sinking. I have seen the sadness on the streets because of this. But the city is not dying, my friends. It is merely returning to God."

While the words that the old man says are fatuous and mean nothing, the people cannot help but be moved. The rich old families from the crumbling houses, those with no religion of their own, nonetheless bow their heads in recognition. Noticing the bowed heads, the old man asks the people to pray, aware that few of them will. He raises his hands briefly, then climbs down the ladder at the back of the stand and disappears from view.

Shortly after he has stepped down, he climbs the ladder again, this time accompanied by a nervous looking girl. She is wearing a simple dress of dark blue, almost black against the grey skies. Carefully, she stands beside him at the top of the stand, pushed forward slightly by his old man's hands. She is thin and frail. It does not matter what her name is, because that has changed now. From this moment, and for the rest of her life, she will be known as Sophia – wisdom. Carefully she is guided into place by the old man, and begins to speak.

"By the crown on my head I will guard you. By this crown the Lord will watch over us. By this crown the mother will guard us. All praise."

She speaks nervously, quickly, and does not allow the crowd enough time to reply in kind.

"I come from among you, and I return to you. This is the worship, this is the way. Remember the city, remember the ocean, remember the forest, remember the life."

The words echo through the loudspeakers. As Joseph listens, he thinks about the night before and his time with Celice. She is a pretty one. He gave her his number. He wonders whether he should call her, or wait for her to call him. Feeling his concentration fade, he tries to focus on the girl standing high there before the cathedral. Gently, she is bowing now and the priest is placing the crown on her head. It is a very thin band of silver, an almost unnoticeable glint in the light.

The moment that the new Queen raises her head, a cheer runs across the crowd from front to back. It is a confused cheer, as though the people are uncertain whether to be jubilant or respectful. When she smiles, the cheer changes to one of delight, loud and sure. After a short time standing there high above the crowd, she takes the old man's hand and cautiously begins to climb down the ladder to the ground.

The new Queen will spend the next couple of hours walking around the crowd, shaking hands and meeting people. Now that her family have been given money, she will have no special privileges. She will return home and live her normal life, and when this week is done she will return to work with the rest of them. All that will remain to mark what has happened is the thin crown on her hair, which she must wear from morning to night. As of now, also, for one year she is married to the city.

When he was younger, Joseph would stay around to meet the new Queen every year. Later, a policeman, he would stand here pressing his gun against his hip, feeling its coldness through the cloth of his pocket. Even when he was serving, he enjoyed the day. It is a trace of excitement, a combining of democracy and worship that he has always liked. Today he has no time for this. The darkness will be coming soon, and the night will be one of excitement. He can see that the coals here are already being set up for the fire-walkers who come later. Taking one last look at the people of the parade, he turns and begins to walk home. He does not travel on the rivers, although it would be quicker. He wants to look at the city slowly and have time to think, as he prepares for meeting Celice this evening and for what might happen.

There is a clear dividing line between the old city and the new. For centuries, Galata was kept enclosed by low walls to the west, away from the sea. As though they were pretending to live on an island, the people limited their living space, afraid that if the city grew too far away from the ocean it would lose its name. It would no longer be the city of rivers. Although that wall ceased to have such desperate significance more than two hundred years ago, as we have already seen the higher up homes are cheaper, uglier and more modern. One thing that excites Joseph terrifically about Celice is that her apartment, to which he has never been, overlooks the water.

When he gets back to his building, after a slow dull climb, Joseph is pleased to find that there is a message on his answerphone. It is Celice. At first he is worried by the clipped distance in the tone of her voice. The message is friendly, however, and the time that it was recorded suggests she must have been suffering from last night's drinking when she phoned. Will he come over, she asks, to a party at her apartment this evening. An informal gathering, she calls it. Quickly, she rattles off her address:

Floor Three
12, Ha-Mayim

The party starts at seven, she says. Later they could go and see the fire-walking? Don't bother to call to confirm. Just come.

The time is a little after four, and it is almost dark outside but not quite. Joseph lights a cigarette and stands out on his small balcony, little more than a thin band of stone hemmed in by metal. There is enough room to stand there, not to sit. He smokes slowly, with his head tilted away from the wind and towards the last of the dusk. As the sky deepens into night and the stars begin to appear, he can hear the first firecrackers lit by children in the streets. The sounds will only get louder as the evening goes on. He spends some time choosing what clothes to wear, although he does not try to iron them. Then he rubs his hands, closes his eyes for a moment to try and see Celice, and – repeating her address over and over to himself – slams the door shut and makes his way down to the ground floor.

Ha-Mayim street backs onto a canal, but the fronts of the houses are on a narrow road. Many of the house-numbers here, those that have endured, are still in gold leaf as they have been for almost two hundred years. These are kept behind glass now, like museum pieces, to prevent thievery. Some houses have no gold numbers; some numbers were peeled off by people desperate for money, during the last war. Joseph is pleased to see that Celice's building still keeps the traditional gold curlicues. He presses the buzzer for floor three, and is disappointed when the voice of a man answers.

"Password!" the voice calls. Behind it are shrieks of laughter and chatter, music. Prepared to greet Celice with a few carefully planned words, Joseph is thrown by hearing the man.

"I'm here for the party," he says, trying to make his voice sound cheerful and drunken.

"Password. Come on. I haven't got all night."

Joseph stalls. Before he has time to answer, the intercom buzzes off. He presses the button and waits again.

"Password!"

Again there is laughter, although less. The joke is wearing thin.

"Celice invited me," says Joseph.

"No Celice here."

"I'm sorry?"

"Just kidding. She's not back yet. Should be back soon. Come in, come in."

There is another, lower buzz and Joseph pushes the door open. The house is so old that there is no space for an elevator, and he climbs the stairs slowly. There is music coming from the second floor. He continues to the third, where more music is playing. Here the door is wide open, propped by a few hardback books. A light haired, fat man is just inside, still standing at the intercom. Behind him are several women in their twenties, none particularly beautiful, all dressed as princesses. The light haired man hands him a plastic glass of red wine.

"S'all we got," he says. "Plenty of red wine. Nothing else. I drank all the beer. Did you bring any beer?"

Joseph curses his stupidity. Of course he should have brought drink. He reaches into his pocket and pulls out a note.

"Here's a contribution," he says.

"Don't be ridiculous. I was kidding. Joke. Understand?"

He reaches out a hand.

"I'm Paul. People call me Fat Paul. You are to call me Paul. You got that?"

Joseph nods.

"Joseph."

Not fat Joseph.

✝

From everything that Celice had told him the day before, Joseph had assumed that she lived alone. She had not mentioned any flat-mates. She was perhaps embarrassed. It soon becomes clear that she and Paul share a large apartment. They have separate rooms, which immediately relieves Joseph. There is no sign that they are lovers, although there is no sign too that Paul knows where Celice was last night. Joseph keeps silent just in case. Whoever Paul is, it is clear that he knows a lot of women. There are perhaps forty people at this party already, and most of them are women dressed as princesses. Also there are some men in smart suits, and one very camp man dressed as a princess. There is always one, and they always think they're unique. Joseph is surprised to find that when he asks any of them how they know Celice, they look at him blankly.

"Oh," say the women. "I don't think I've met her. Does she live here?"

"Celice?" say the men, tapping the side of their glasses with thin fingers, looking embarrassed and confused. Then they ask one of the women, and the woman shakes her head. It seems no-one here has met her. For hours she does not turn up. Eventually, Joseph becomes bored of standing on his own or trying to charm women who do not interest him, and he hunts out Paul.

"Any idea when Celice might be back?"

"She comes and goes," says Paul. "You know how it is. Men, women. I can't fathom them. I can't even fathom her. Can't even fathom my own damned sister."

Although this is not precisely the answer Joseph wants to hear, he smiles. So that's why they live together.

"Sister?"

"Well. By marriage. Second marriage. All dead now. God. Rest. Their. Souls."

He says this very slowly, ironically, one flat palm thumping the wall with every word.

"They moved in with us when she was two, so I think of her like that. A stupid sister. She's always somewhere. I don't worry about it. Don't think I want to live with her. She definitely doesn't want to live with me. She'll turn up. Drink."

This is not a question. Joseph drinks more wine. He is drinking very fast and soon he loses track of the time. He is tempted to pretend he is looking for the bathroom, and stumble upon Celice's room. That feels too invasive, so he drinks more and eventually does go for a piss. He stays in the bathroom for a while, with his head leaning against the mirror, trying to pull himself back from the brink of sickness. When he comes back, there are fewer people in the room. Soon Paul walks up to him.

"It's eleven, Jo-Jo," he says. "Fire-walking time. Your feet ready for it?"

Joseph laughs.

"I'd rather watch."

"You and me both. Celice, she likes that sort of junk. Probably down there already." He looks at Joseph and realises drunkenly that the man in front of him is disappointed. "Come on. She'll be there."

Ushering the rest of the guests out of the room, he guides Joseph down the stairs and they make their way out into the damp air.

It is not quite raining when they leave Ha-Mayim street, but as the group walk along the narrow pavement it begins to drizzle. Some people have left their homes without their shoes, because of the fire-walking, and they are regretting it now. Soon they will be grateful for the rain, because water on the ground makes the brief dash over coals far easier. For now they are shivering.

This fire-walking is the last event that happens every year. As of tomorrow, all of the events are devised only for every hundredth year – and, more particularly, for this thousandth year. Some people, the rich, have set up their own fires in long gardens. Most go back to the central square, where Sophia was crowned earlier. There, ten metre long lines of fire that were lit at eight have been reduced now to smoking coals. It is a ritual, a ceremony. There's no point in taking unnecessary risks. But the notion is that anyone who dares to walk or run across the flames, or what remains of them, will have good fortune for the whole year. This must be done during the chimes that ring on New Year's Day. Otherwise it is worthless.

By the time Joseph and Paul have reached the square, it is already almost a quarter to twelve. As soon as they get there, Joseph lets out a whoop of delight and recognition.

"Erin," he says, calling to a woman standing near the flames, getting ready to get in line. "How's the art world?"

It turns out that Erin is an artist and that Joseph has seen her works. In her words, she 'creates spaces', and one of those spaces was created near Joseph's parents' old house. She had strung a whole street across with lines of silver string, and called it 'temporary migration'. Joseph hadn't thought much of it. The plan had been for birds to rest there, and they had, encouraged in particular by a scattering of seed that she and others had placed there around dawn each morning. What Erin hadn't thought about was the fact that birds shit, and within weeks the whole street had been peppered with white spots. People had protested, Joseph's parents for one, and it had been taken down.

The temporary distraction of meeting the person responsible for this makes him forget about Celice. He also forgets about her because Erin is very beautiful. He nods in appreciation at her ridiculous ideas. He has to, because she doesn't seem even faintly interested in his own. She continues to be fascinated by birds, she says. This is appropriate because she looks like a bird; the sort of neurotic girl who never eats, who is trying to make her bones hollow with fasting. She plans now to thread strings between two bridges. She wants to call it 'Flight on the water'. The council won't let her. They are terrible people.

She speaks very quickly. Carefully, Paul leaves Joseph with her and goes to talk to other friends. Soon five minutes have passed, and Joseph finds himself standing in line with her behind one of the fires, looking at the policemen on the corners. He doesn't recognise one of them.

"You've got to take off your shoes," Erin says. Still very drunk, and giddy with the stupid ideas from the woman's mind, he pulls off his shoes and holds them in one hand. He has never done this before, but this seems a good opportunity. He wants to impress. And so, when the bishop appears on the stand again one minute before the chimes, he is ready.

"Walk on fire. Walk on water. All is possible with the Lord."

The bishop says no more, but the drums start then and the people start repeating it as a mantra. Most people are standing at the edges of the square watching those who have volunteered themselves for fire-walking. Erin feels for Joseph's hand.

"Let's do it together," she says. The melody that precedes the chimes begins ringing. The high-up bells rattle it out. Joseph reaches for spaces between the notes, but there are none. And then the chimes begin, and Erin has taken his hand, and they are running.

The fire-walking is nothing much. There are many people ahead of them, and the moisture on their feet has damped down the heat to almost nothing by the time they reach the coals. Still it is an invigorating experience. They are surrounded by people cheering, and when they reach the other end of the fire they are led off by figures standing there and given glasses of hot spirit. Soon Erin takes off her crown and beckons to Joseph to do the same. He has forgotten he is wearing the tinny thing, light on his hair, but when he realises he removes it. They exchange their crowns and Erin gives him a kiss on the cheek then turns away.

"Don't be a stranger," she says as she leaves.

When she has gone, there is no-one who Joseph recognises here, which is unsurprising. Most of his old friends have children, young children. They will be at home in bed, sleeping or talking to their lovers about what they will do tomorrow. Joseph can remember a time when he would have recognised one in ten people here. That time is gone; everyone is younger or older. The policemen he used to serve with are mostly in offices now. His other friends, those with young children, have had to go to bed.

Being left alone makes Joseph realise once more that the whole point of the evening has failed. He has not met up with Celice. He will not be sleeping with her. Without the energy even to sigh, he begins the slow walk home, holding the tatty crown in his hands. On his journey home he walks as much by the canals as he can. Still very drunk, he likes the sway of the water because it settles him. Eventually he has to cut onto the dry roads and make his way up the slope to his road. He goes in, gets in the elevator, whirrs upstairs and pours himself a large glass of water. The taste of it is unpleasant, as though it has lived too long in the pipes. But metal in your water, he has heard, protects you from disease.

None of the people from the party know where Joseph lives. That is the first thing he realises when he wakes, and he is sad of that. Because Celice did not show the night before, he is embarrassed to go back there without an invitation. This is a shame because they seem like fun people and he would rather spend the rest of the week with them than with his old friends and their children.

The cafes, fortunately, are open this week even if the rest of the city is not. He goes out and orders himself a coffee at the nearest, sitting inside but near enough the window that he can see the shadows from the plane trees spilling down onto the ground. The café is filled with people cradling their heads and reading newspapers. In the end, when a woman leaves her table, he is able to take one of the papers for his own. It is a morning special and almost everything in it talks about the festival. He reads it through but he does not find the little article a junior journalist has written about Celice. There are always bodies being found in the canals, after all.

Chapter Two.

The crowd had gathered around the body in a peculiar way
– a way that is peculiar to bodies that are found in water. It,
for we shall no longer call it she, was first seen floating early
in the morning. The first to see her was a long boat taking
drunks home. By then the pilot of the boat was also a little
drunk. All night he had been swigging from a whiskey
bottle. There were a lot of collisions between boats that
night, but the only collision he had was with a corpse.

The collision did not sober him, but he was together
enough to almost steer a boat and together enough to know
what he had just seen. At the next stop, he told everyone to
get off and roped the boat to the water's edge. He then
called the river police, who came soon with nets. They
pulled the body in at the edge of Bekorah street. That was
what often happened. It is easier to say that bodies are
washed up, in the press, but very often they are pulled in.

Crowds watching a horrific spectacle are both fascinated
and afraid. There was only a thin space here, but the small
crowd that gathered managed to show both traits. They
approached the netting and the corpse with a combination
of distance and closeness. They clamoured, but stopped
some way away, the outline of the crowd curved in the way
that swarms of locusts curve against an opposing wind.
Women stood nearest the front and men looked over them.
The body was clean and only a little bruised. Its hair was
wet and it was a little bloated from the saltwater. There was
a pallor to it that was reminiscent of salt. Only the most
ambitious of poets would have dared to call it beautiful.

Soon the police declared there was nothing to see, and
soon after that there really was nothing to see. The body
was wrapped up in a cloth bag that had been treated to
protect it against water damage. A few policemen stood
over it. One, a thin-boned man with grey hair, held a
cigarette in his long fingers. He wanted to call this suicide

because it seemed a shame to spoil the celebrations with the threat of a murder. He didn't want to frighten people. Because of that the body was not searched until it finally reached the morgue. The papers had been wrapped in tin foil, as though to keep them dry, but by then they were still pretty much mush. J. D., though, saw fairly soon there was something remarkable about them. The message was illegible but whatever it had been the paper was burned at the edges, as though it had been important for this message to be surrounded for a moment by flames. J. D. was surprised for a moment then afraid. He had started on forensic because he was good at it, and also because he was fascinated by it. And he was now very much aware that something like this – the body, the paper, the charring at the edges – hadn't been washed up anywhere for something like a hundred years. For exactly a hundred years.

Fat Paul woke with a head that hated him and looked around the room. It hadn't cleaned itself while he was asleep, he was disappointed to see. Taking a swig from a bottle of flat, false champagne, he slumped out of bed in his underwear and walked on shaky legs through to the living room. All the women were gone, although the man dressed as a princess still lay on the floor. Paul kicked his head half-heartedly a few times, and the man stirred and then started snoring once more. Still no sign of Celice. No matter. She was often gone for days.

It was inconsiderate of her, though, to disappear before the party.

Paul knew even less about Celice than most people know about their brothers or sisters. She was a burden. She refused to work. Since Paul refused to work too, this would have been an impossible strain if it hadn't been for the kindness of the state and these inherited rooms. Paul wouldn't have minded the fact that she refused to work. He was easy going, and most of his friends were self-righteous artists who thought they were going somewhere and kept

themselves unemployed in their struggle to create. What he minded was the arrogant certainty with which Celice carried herself. The blank way in which she fielded his questions whenever she went out. She was studying in the evenings, she said. Couldn't they just leave it at that?

A man with no secrets, Paul found secrecy very irritating. It was not something that intrigued him. It just bored him. Secrets were a way of pretending you were more than you were. Celice hadn't always been that way. But ever since turning twenty-one, she had become stupidly secretive. She disappeared for nights on end. Paul derived some entertainment out of this, when he spoke to the few friends he had who knew her.

It was boring. She would always come back with nothing; no pictures, no art, no stories. Nothing worthwhile at all. She would walk in through the door after days of absence, make some kind of herbal tea and sit down on the sofa. She would look at Paul as though she were challenging him to ask her questions. But if he ever did, he only met with the same blankness. If they could get Celice to hold back the waters, Paul thought, maybe this city wouldn't be in such a desperate state. She was very good at keeping things at a distance.

Circles are everywhere. The sun, of course, is a circle. At this moment Joseph is sitting in the café, planning his day and looking up at the sun. He has reached the back page of the paper and he has been reading the schedule. Normally there would be sports here, but there are no sports this week, or if there are then the newspaper has decided they don't matter. He reads the schedule for some time, then he looks up at the sun, trying to decipher the circle through the branches of the tree. Like many trees here, it looks unhealthy because of the salt they can't split from the soil. But it is tall, and its branches are fairly strong. Joseph is playing the game of catching sunlight, then gazing off into shadow and still watching the pock-marks of dullness and blindness that the sun has left in his eyes. They fade after a while.

The schedule is interesting. There are fewer parades today, but those that there are should be intriguing, he supposes. The whole of this week is a time of transformation. Every day the transformations are different, working up to the end of the week when they should be quite wonderful. Today, after the fire and fury of last night, the parades and the costumes have started at the other end of the spectrum. Today the only transformation that the people are making is into a sort of parody of themselves. This is a day for working people. They will band themselves into groups, dressed in the clothes of their trade, and they will march up and down celebrating their jobs. It seems a ridiculous thing to celebrate. There will be marches of butchers, of bakers. Probably even candlestick-makers. The first marches started early. Later, Joseph reads, the different trades should be grouping together towards the centre of the city. Perhaps, he thinks, his old friends will be there. Policemen, all dressed up, trying to be friendly as they march along. The thought entertains him briefly. He leaves a tip and begins to wander down.

As he walks, Joseph is amused to see how far the city has become public property for the week. People everywhere are doing things that commonly no-one would be allowed to do. Those police who are not on the march let their guns hang loose in their holsters. Nothing much interests them. Parents and children are walking the old streets, where the statues are. They are wrapping the faces of ancient statues – statues commissioned by the Manvilles, statues by great and classic artists like Dubois and Gallucci – with tin foil. They are taking death-masks of these statues, lifting them off as carefully as a mother lifts a child. These are to take home. It is even possible to buy the masks. Some people are too lazy to do it themselves, and poor children are making a killing out of spreading the masks out onto dry rugs and selling them for whatever they can get. Rich women are carrying the masks around cautiously, desperate not to break their shape before they get them home.

Gargoyles, or Marys, or Christs. The classic face of David, blank eyed and pure.

"Masks of the city. Get them while you can."

People are touching statues that it would have been a crime to approach two days ago. Cordons and ropes are down all round the city. At one point, walking down Hanahash Street, Joseph is approached by a man selling rolls of tin foil for a ludicrous amount of money. People are paying it. People are desperate to take a record while they can. Most of these masks will buckle and fold, of course. The only way to make a good, true death mask is from plaster of Paris. Perhaps if the faces were covered over and over with the foil, until the metal grew stiff and hard to alter, they might endure. The faces that most people are creating will just break apart given a gust of wind.

Joseph is not quite sure what the job of the police is, this week. They are smiling when they are seen, and in fact hardly any of them are seen here, some distance from Elohim. Most of the police are in their own parade now, dressed in their best regalia, calling one another brother, patting each other on the back and laughing about how many people they've killed. He wishes he could have joined up again, just for the week, in a way. He scratches at the scar on his left arm, and smiles. It's all for the best.

Thinking of the parade, Joseph begins a more concerted walk towards the centre. Perhaps the tradesmen will be giving out free food, he thinks. As he walks, he looks up at the great salt-stained pictures of old. They are lovely. He is glad to think that haloes are high up, because the hems of the gowns in the paintings are faded from where the high waters have lapped through the streets. People are taking advantage of the loose rules of the week to approach any painting that they like. To run their hands across the faces, to stroke the ancient breasts of beautiful women with their heads hung modest over stone. Joseph looks at the haloes surrounding the faces of these perfect pictures corrupted by time. They are perfect circles, and though the gold leaf elsewhere has been stolen across the ages, most of the haloes are left intact. They glint and reflect the light like second suns.

The writing on the paper that was found on Celice's body was found close to her breast, where her heart would have nurtured it if her heart had just kept beating. While it has been wrapped in foil to protect it from water damage, it is nonetheless now completely unreadable, but that does not mean that J. D. can't tell that it is print from a notebook, a very old one. They used higher quality paper a hundred years ago, two hundred years ago. The cheap pulp of modern notebooks would have crumbled into nothing much in the water. He takes the paper mass, singed into a circle, and – wearing thin plastic gloves throughout – he spreads it onto a stone table in the centre of the room. Then he switches on the bright light above that is normally used for examining wounds. There is nothing much to see. Someone somewhere has burned the paper. Maybe it was Celice, although judging from the bruises across her body and the sharp cut and swell just above her hairline, J. D. thinks it unlikely. The water has, of course, destroyed all fingerprints.

After examining the paper for a long time, J. D. goes out of the room, locking it as he does so. The rest of the police station is almost deserted. He goes into the silent canteen and presses a button to get himself a coffee. It bubbles up, dried milk and coffee crumbling down into boiling water. After he has drunk his coffee he makes his way back to the office. There is no point going home. His children and wife are out at the celebrations. He goes into the study adjacent to the forensic room and walks up and down until he finds the right book. Then he pulls it down and thumps it flat on the floor with the manner of a man who has forgotten about sleep. He has almost two hundred of these books. Forensic records for every year. Quite a library.

January 1. The body of a young woman. Notable features: black hair, blue eyes. Water damage, swollen tongue. Approx. time of death: 03:00 am. Silver rings, two. Some

broken teeth. Arms were folded neatly when found. Some bruising, signs of damage, but no signs of struggle. Papers found on body. Unreadable, but looks like verse? Burned at edges in a regular manner. Cause of death: inconclusive.

The writing before him is old, blue fountain-pen ink on yellowing paper. Quickly he thumbs through the pages.

January 2. Young woman. Approx. time of death: uncertain. No wounds, some salt damage. Arms were folded neatly when found. Papers found on body. Burned at edges in regular manner. Some words legible. 'Water ... Sun and Hope ... ' Cause of death: probable suicide.

There is a record like this for every day. Every day for one week, exactly one hundred years ago. J. D. sighs, then lifts himself from the ground, straining his exhausted muscles. He just prays that the press don't get hold of this. He knows from bitter experience how much of a fuss the papers can make about these things.

The fact that the writing is unreadable, that the words have streaked together, would seem to render the paper completely useless. Many people would just throw it away now. Many of J. D.'s colleagues would have done so. But none of them are there; they are all out at the festivities. Carefully, J. D. lifts the clump of paper up to the light and turns it from side to side. The ink is impossibly smudged, but while the water has smeared away a lot of things, it has also kept something. In the tin foil that had wrapped the paper, the shadow of some very light markings shows here. J. D. can't take a rubbing; the foil is too brittle for that. But turning it from side to side, he can make out the vague indent of a phone number. It is a number he recognises, one he hasn't dialled for a couple of years. He takes a couple of photographs, the camera-eye opened wide to let in the light. He writes it down for safe-keeping. He likes to write everything down.

Near the centre, children are taking bark rubbings of trees, or rubbings of street-numbers, going over and over paper with wax crayons. Everyone is active except for the very old. For the first time in a long time Joseph misses his family. He misses the old house down in the centre of town, down Keruvim street. Although he has been thinking of going to see the March of the Merchants, today's great festivity, he suddenly decides seeing all the different professions will only make him sad. He enjoys not having to work, but it is hard not being able to belong. Instead he turns to make his way to Keruvim street. It is a street that tourists reach by river, but Joseph knows the subtle alleyways. He walks close to one side in the alleyways, avoiding much of the rain that is blowing in at a slant from the sea. Some of those who are intending to attend the march are in the alleyways. People dressed up as parodies of butchers, accountants, chefs. Joseph ignores them. He is going back to his old house. He is going home.

When he reaches Keruvim street Joseph closes his eyes and counts the steps to the house, opening his eyes now and again to check where he is. As always he reaches the house faster than he thought he would. It is a tall beautiful building, in the street of the Cherubim. His mother and father have been dead for three years now. He'd heard about his father from his hospital bed, while he'd been recovering from the gunshot wound. His mother had nursed Joseph for a month after that, and then he'd nursed her for three more until she died. Then he'd sold the house abruptly to someone old, who did not care that it was sinking into the sea. He quit his job and took the money. Joseph is not as poor as he pretends to be. He owns nowhere, his possessions are few, but he will never want as long as he is frugal. He will live here for a few years, he thinks. Then it will be time to leave. But so far, it has never quite been time to leave.

There is graffiti in this neighbourhood now. This is

something new. There were always the tragic little daubs of kids. Now, though, the graffiti has taken on the quality of art. People have started leaving graffiti artists alone while they paint, and because of that their pictures have taken on a richer texture and far more detail than ever before. As Joseph sits on the steps of his old home, pretending to himself that he owns it, he looks at the shop window opposite and smiles to see that it has been painted over. The shop closed a long time ago, but the artist, whoever it was, has created a false front with old-text messages. At first sight it looks like an old-fashioned chemist. Closer-to, it becomes evident that the drugs on offer are all illegal.

Joseph is tempted to stay sitting there in the shade all day. The old man who lives in his house seems to be out. Very few people are around. He kicks his heels against the step over and over again. The people he sees are a strange combination. There are the new rich, with their flamboyant clothing and their absence of care. There are the old, then. But Joseph notices that there are no children in the street at all. It has become inhabited only by people with money to burn, or people with little time left. He can remember the first time the waters reached this far. He had been seven years old. The middle of winter. He had taken the change from out of his pockets, and cast it again and again into the waterlogged streets. Then he had pretended to himself that he was finding it once more beneath the thin shimmer of water. It seems a shame that there are no children left, but he can understand why. There are fewer families with children anywhere in the city, nowadays. He shouldn't suppose his old street would be any different.

At the local cafeteria, the tables have also been daubed with graffiti. This is less interesting stuff; the common taunts and jeers, the familiar declarations of love in thick marker pen, the occasional circle with initials inside. The man who owns the cafeteria is nowhere to be seen, but when the waitress comes she is young enough and plain enough that Joseph feels comfortable asking her about this.

"I don't know," says the waitress. "Every day we used to clean it off. But nowadays... well, it gets impossible. The kids come in on Fridays, Saturdays. They come here for coffees, you know. After they've been drinking. They spend a lot. They like to draw stuff. Doesn't seem much point scrubbing away at it, really. It only comes back again."

"So, what? Is anyone allowed to just draw what they want?"

"It's not my job to tell them not to. Now, what's your order?"

Because she is neither attractive nor charming and he doesn't want to appear prejudiced, Joseph tips the waitress over the odds before he leaves. The bacon-fat from his sandwich is heavy in his stomach, but he is smiling as he makes his way away. Before he left, he took out a pen of his own and wrote. Nothing much, just his initials and the date. That seems to be what most people like to leave.

Still staying away from the centre and the main body of the parade, Joseph walks back up to his apartment through the streets. There are a few birds that he likes to look at and then chase away. He is still feeling slightly sick and sad about going home and perhaps that is an excuse for his childish behaviour. When he does reach home he doesn't notice the grey-haired man sitting opposite his apartment; he's too busy fumbling for his keys. J. D. gives him some time to enter, then leaves it a little while longer. When he sees Joseph click open the doors to his balcony, he realises that he has gone into the right apartment. He buzzes the door and waits.

"Joseph Cramer?"

"Speaking."

"Can I come in?"

"What do you want to sell me?"

"Nothing. Look, it's John Douglas. Remember?"

"Come on up."

J. D. looks at the old caged lift for a moment warily, then begins the slow climb up the stairs. The door is already open, and he lumbers in, leaning for a moment against the wall as Joseph looks at him. He's surprised to see the greyness of J. D.'s hair.

"Christ, J. D. You've been wearing yourself thin."

The man in front of him has that look, like thinly spread margarine. He's pale and exhausted and the low light through the window makes him seem even more pale than he is. J. D. tries to smile at his old associate, a man he hasn't seen for a couple of years. Might as well be friendly. He looks around him. There's no television, but he's not surprised at that. There's never anything worth watching on anyway these days. There are some old pictures, a few books. Some cigarette packets scattered here and there. Too many tissues, used and otherwise. He sits down on the sofa uninvited, and looks up at the thin man in front of him.

"I take it you're not here to ask me back on the force," says Joseph.

"Not exactly, Joseph. I was just reminded of you this morning, and I thought I'd call by. Your number was given to me. Well, I should say it was found. On the body of a woman. It seems she partied a little too hard."

There seems no point giving the gruesome details now.

"Whatever happened, she was found washed up this morning. Didn't have any other details on her, but she had your number. I recognised your number, got your address. I hope you don't mind. It seemed like it was important. Do you mind if I smoke?"

Surprised, Joseph shakes his head and gives the grey-haired man an old cup to collect ash. J. D. takes out a cigarette with a crabbed movement that suggests arthritis. He had decided before leaving the office that Joseph was certainly not a killer, and though the worn face before him is one that's changed since leaving the force, he doesn't think it's changed that much. Upon showing a polaroid of the body's face to Joseph, he's not at all surprised to discover that he doesn't even know its surname.

"I met her the day before New Year's," Joseph says. "She gave me her number." He pours a couple of pitchers of rum, filling them up to the top to show that he's not as poor as his rooms suggest.

"Well, it appears you gave her yours as well. Perhaps you could tell me a little more about her. Profession?"

"I don't have one."

J. D. doesn't laugh, although Joseph's fairly proud of the joke.

"Hers."

Joseph thinks about what Celice had told him, two nights before.

"She called herself an artist."

J. D. shakes his head. Doesn't everyone, nowadays?

"No real help there, then. What else do you have?"

With his hands shaking a little from shock, Joseph walks to the answerphone and rewinds it. Both are silent as they listen to it whirr, then click into action. An address. 12, Ha-Mayim. A nice area. It's old, the trees on the streets are tall.

"She lives with her brother," he says. "Lived."

He reaches for the cigarettes on the table and takes one for himself.

"Well, I'd better get onto him. Do you know where he was last night?"

Joseph thinks of the fat figure lumbering around to music, or smoking cannabis on the balcony with the gay man.

"At the party. We were all at the party. I mean, I was."

"Right. Are you doing anything at the moment?"

"I was drinking rum. Look, do I have to be a part of this?"

"Only if you want to. It would be nice to have someone to lead the way."

Joseph smiles, then shrugs. He wishes now that the drink he had bought had been more expensive. He doesn't like to have guests, but when he does he doesn't like to let them down. He crunches the ice, feels the pain of the cold against his back teeth.

"OK," he says with a sigh. He finishes his drink, and the last from the other glass, and guides J. D. out of the room with his left hand. Together they walk down the stairs, avoiding the lift again.

"I don't really like caged lifts."

"You and me both. Do you want to examine the body first?"

"It would be nice to see her again."

The first thing Joseph asks when they reach the station is that J. D. cover the body, which lies naked on the examining table. While he has seen many dead naked women in his time – hysterical suicide is quite frequent here, with so many places in which to drown – it seems inappropriate to gaze at the corpse of a girl he kissed so recently. Quickly, J. D. covers it with a blanket, leaving the face plain to see. Joseph runs his hand against the face, feeling the cut and the swell. The room is very cold, colder even than outside. It postpones decay. When he has finished looking and touching her face, J. D. leads him over and into his study. He closes the door and switches on the heater and pulls down the records he had before. Joseph reads them with a kind of rapture that even he knows is inappropriate. He has missed this part of the job; the facts, the details. He missed it far more than the killing.

It takes Joseph half an hour of silent reading before he is ready to stop. He reads the notes over and over. First one woman, then another. Seven days, seven deaths. Seven brides for seven rivers. The case is an odd one, one which he himself remembers with affection. There was always something delightful in reading about unsolved crimes, as long as they happened long enough ago for them to be well and truly over. It was a way to pass the time, and he had liked the thought of his forebears being outwitted. J. D. brings him some coffee, which draws him back a little from the drunken distance he had managed to achieve. The details are fascinating. Some are clearly murders; some seem as clearly to be suicides.

"Take this one," says J. D. "Poppy Fields. Pretty name."

"Pretty."

"Well, it's one of the few names we've got. Four of the seven, they never found their names. But Poppy – well, she was a rich girl. Daddy's little pet. Got herself involved in something. Very interested in art, romance. Her dad owned part of the gallery on Sha-Mayim street. Then she was found washed up, carrying nothing on her but a clump of charred paper. No damage. They only recognised the body by a tattoo. A butterfly, a little way above the hip. Or take this. Alicia Fields. Sister of the deceased. Deceased too, on the fourth day. A blow to the head did for her."

"To lose two children seems like carelessness…"

"Well, the Fields never recovered. Gave it all up, donated their garden to the city. That's Sha-Mayim Park, now. The other one, she wasn't related. But it seems like they knew each other. They were artists, or artist's models, all of them. They tried to pin the murders on the painter, but he always had an alibi. He made quite a lot of money out of it, actually. Not much of an artist, but the death of the subject always knocks a picture's price up."

J. D. smiles as he takes up the book, closes it and puts it neatly back on the shelf. For a moment Joseph is pleased for the man, who has clearly found somewhere to settle. He remembers how he liked working with him. The aversion they both had to action; the way they both preferred to stay inside, hiding, avoiding the real world as much as possible. Turning it all into a sort of comfortable fiction.

"It's a fun little old story, this one. Rich kids, getting involved in something. But look. I just wanted to get you in here, before we go to Ha-Mayim street. There's a reason. We've got to tell her brother, or whatever he is. But to be honest, I'm not that eager to. Because I'll be surprised if this is the last time this week we see something like this."

Joseph turns and follows J. D. back into the other room. The clump of old paper is still there, charred around the edges in a near-perfect circle. It sits on the desk in the corner, underneath a standard lamp, resting on a sheet of cellophane to keep it as intact as possible. The smears of ink are completely illegible, almost as though they were written in some ink that was designed to fall into nothingness in water. Joseph sits on the seat, while J. D. stands over by the body and waits. He looks hard at the paper, and wishes he could try to separate the sheets. But he knows if he did, then the whole would just fall into mush.

Writing prayers takes a particular sort of concentration. The moment you make a mistake, the whole is ruined. Using old paper like this is not easy. Blank notebooks from a hundred years ago are relatively hard to come by, almost expensive. Besides, to make a mistake would be a sin, a transgression. He writes carefully and slowly. He says every word while he writes it, and as he writes he says nothing else.

It was a shame to have to wound the other. She had seemed so eager at first. She loved the city, she had said. She loved its paintings, its architecture. She would do anything to keep it from being destroyed. Every teacher loves a willing pupil, and he had taken her at her word. They all had. But then, when the prayers had been prepared in her name, after hours of hard work, she had retracted her claim. Silly, really. For a while, it had seemed like Celice had so much dignity. The problem was, he supposed, that he had let the girl keep the prayer to herself for too long. She had read it over and over. She had taken it away, wrapped in foil, saying it was too beautiful to damage. She had been given time to think. A whole day and night to think. He had thought he was doing her a favour; giving her a chance to contemplate the great sacrifice she was about to make.

That mistake was not going to be made again. The next volunteer was being wined and dined as he wrote. A lovely girl, promising. He always wanted to choose those with some promise. He wrote her name in the spaces prepared in the hymn. He wrote it neatly, with as much care as all of the other words. The precious words, the sacred phrases. He was almost finished when the knock came on his study door, to let him know that she was now asleep. Gently he left the room and, surrounded by the others, he took out a box of matches. She was lying there naked with her arms folded neatly across her chest, her flat palms pointing upwards beneath her chin. She stirred a little as the paper was placed beneath her arms, and when the burning began she almost cried. The drugs were powerful enough in the end to keep her still. He burned all round the edges, patting the flames down when they seemed to be blazing too hard. He was glad he didn't have to kill her before throwing her into the canal. It was much better for all of them if she was just given to the river.

Chapter Three.

Paul is too drunk to be wary when he answers the door – drunk enough that he assumes it is all a joke at first, even the identification papers and the gun strapped against J. D.'s waist. He smiles and he thinks what has that bitch got herself into now and he pours drinks for the two men, one of whom he almost knows. Nobody is ever going to say that Paul Dubois is unfriendly.

J. D. has been in enough of these situations – they both have – not to push the point of the death until after they have received their drinks. It is an exceptionally good bottle of wine, red, and it would be a shame to ruin it by breaking the cork. A shaking hand can ruin the best bottle of wine, and Paul's hands start to shake the moment that he sees the photograph of his sister lain out on a blanket. Yes, he does know her and yes she does live here. Of course they can look into her room, of course. He stands in the doorway as they search the room and look at the photographs and the paintings. He thinks about the bruising on his sister's face and wonders if he will have to see the body, wonders whether she was found naked or if the police stripped her bare before they lay her out to dry.

"She's an artist," he says as the two men look at the pictures on the wall. "Photo-montage. Stinks the place out with chemicals. Like a laboratory or something." He points at the blinds, rolled up now, which can seal out every aspect of light. "Always developing pictures."

"Did you see much of her?"

"Not really. She was in all day, I suppose. I sleep late. Self-employed."

She *was*. Paul, who is accustomed to sadness and loss, rolls the word around his tongue.

"What do you do?"

"I'm a professional drinker."

It comes out before he thinks, the glib answer.

"I mean, I don't do much. My parents – my father. You may have heard of him. Phillipe Dubois?"

"The musician."

"Yes, well…"

J. D. doesn't need to ask more. He has never liked opera, but he knows Phillipe's name from the papers; knows him for his affairs. Knows the famous song, the song that sold – the well-known recording of the *Wave* movement. This fat man, with his shaking hands. He doesn't need to work.

While Joseph and J. D. search the room, Paul walks out and into the kitchen, drinking fast. Although he never felt any shame in searching Celice's room when she might return – searching for cigarettes, attractive photographs of her friends, perhaps nude studies – it feels wrong now. He stands and gazes at his glass and thinks about how her mother stole his father away; about the fact that he has always seen her mother in her face. He was glad when they died, bitter only because he had to share the pickings with the girl. His sister, the little bitch who had come to join them at the age of two, screaming and mewling and getting prettier by the day. Dead now, and the music of the city still going on, the too-close sounds of people down below. She always thought of herself as perfect, he thinks, and that is what he says when the two come out clasping a sheaf of photographs she must have developed herself. He shakes his head as he looks at them.

"I'm surprised she found it in herself to die. She always said she'd never die. She always thought of herself as perfect."

There are seven photographs there. J. D. counts them out as though that were important. All of them are of a woman with dark hair. Tall, if a photograph can make a person seem tall, and pale. But in truth neither he nor anyone else can be certain that the photographs are of Celice. Because in developing them, she has blurred the image carefully all the way around. The faces in the photographs are blurred into almost nothing, just dark eyes and the curve of a mouth and the hair swept back. And all around the face there lies the circled weight of a halo, blurring the image

more. It's a simple photographer's trick, crude. Parts of the paper were exposed to light, and parts were most definitely not. The end result is this pure halo, swept around a barely-discernable face.

J. D. searches the room for an hour or more, always accepting wine when it is offered. The festival is continuing into the night and it is a drunken one. He finds negatives for simple studies, flowers and sunsets, but no negatives for these pictures. In the end he takes the pictures and thanks Paul and asks him if he know anything about where Celice has gone after dark, during those hours when he has been drinking with friends. He shrugs, too far gone to say much. She does courses, he says. Monday to Friday, she's always busy. Never brings friends home, never talks to him about much, only about money. Soon J. D. gets out a notebook and starts to write down the pointless ramblings of the drunk man, who veers now between laughter and near-tears. As he writes, Joseph flicks through the photographs over and over. Although the technique used is simple, there is something very beautiful about the way they have been made, the way that almost all of the face has been smoothed away. It is still definitely a face, he sees, a woman surrounded by the smear of a halo. And yet, it could be anyone.

Fat Paul offers himself so willingly to J. D. that he knows he cannot know anything much. The questions he asks are simple and blunt and the answers he gets are almost empty. Joseph can believe that Paul knows little about his sister's life, about the life of this woman to whom he wasn't even related by blood. They have shared together for four years, since his father's death. Her mother died before him, but still Paul's father left the apartment to them both. He's sorry to hear of her death, he says, but he won't be crying over it. The girl was nothing much to do with him, and her dying is none of his business.

Paul has no addresses to offer them and a search of the

room gives no details, only pictures of flowers and trees. There are no other photographs of people beside the seven of the dark-haired woman, still freshly developed and stinking of chemicals but stripped of any negatives. Eventually the pair leave the drunk man, warning him that he must not leave the city until their investigations are done.

"I haven't left the city in twenty years," says Paul as though he is proud of this. "I'm not about to start now."

Outside the street is dark apart from the lamps, white here in the centre. All of the street-lamps in the old town are white light, while those in the suburbs are orange. It makes the streets here seem more calm, and somehow it often encourages silence. Tonight the streets are not silent; they are busy with people still commemorating their trades. Joseph and J. D. look at them gathering in groups at the street corners. There is one group of students, adults, perhaps eighteen or nineteen. The women are dressed as though they were far younger; dressed like school-girls with their hair in bunches and their skirts hauled high against their knees. There are other trades too, everywhere – maids and teachers and workmen and bank-clerks, all dressed like erotic parodies of themselves now it is dark. The children are gone and everyone else is getting ready for the night. J. D. shakes his head in disapproval as they walk through the streets and back to the police-station.

At the station the two of them drink coffee and ignore the fact there is a dead woman in the next room, not even looking towards the closed metal door. They talk about old times, although both of them are thinking at the back of their minds about the present. There is no-one there when they arrive, but half-way through the second cup of coffee – when both of them are buzzing from the pressure of caffeine – a thin, weasel-faced man marches in from the coldroom with the stiff sad march of someone who is used to being bullied.

"J. D."

Even his voice is weak.

"Ah, Ronald. Not at the march?"

J. D. knows why without asking. First, Ronald Andersen is not someone who people like to be around. He is the police's chief pathologist, and being around someone who is so fond of death is a little repellent to most people. Second, Andersen far prefers the company of corpses. They don't answer back, as he has said before in a drunken moment, and besides they are cleaner than most people, at least at first. He sees to that himself. Once again, J. D. wonders to himself whether Andersen has ever seen a living naked woman. He is never happier than when there is a fresh body to examine, a body that he can cluck over in sorrow and clean with alcohol in the chilly room next door.

"I'm too busy for such nonsense," Andersen says with a self-important air. "Don't these idiots know there's a murder been committed? I came as soon as I got your message. I was surprised that you weren't here, to be honest. There was so much still to be seen to with the body."

"I had other people to see, Andersen. Living ones."

The thin man gives a nervous laugh.

"Well, yes. I see. Joseph, isn't it? Not a policeman any more, are you. But since we're among friends, I suppose I can share. After all, this was a fascinating one."

He rubs his hands together, red hands that are chapped and sore with alcohol-burns.

"I suppose you've both seen the bruises, but there's more than just that. The fact is … " He shrugs. "It takes a chemist's eye to see it. It takes an analytical mind to realise it, J. D. You don't need to feel ashamed for not noticing. It's not your province, after all. You walk the streets, don't you."

Andersen says this in a snide way, as though J. D. were a prostitute.

"Anyway, I did the complete analysis."

"A fine-toothed comb?"

"Far better than that. I used my eyes, J. D. They don't miss a thing. And there was something about her hair that I noticed."

The way that Andersen talks makes Joseph want to gag,

and he's glad for the first time that evening that he's left the force. He never minded the people who did the job for money, who had to do it and had nowhere else to go, like John Douglas. But he always hated the scientists, the analysts; people who revelled in their job. He thinks about the number of times he's stood in this room listening to Andersen talking about the dead like this, calling them angels and beauties and darlings like some mad old woman talking about a handsome boy.

Andersen claps his palms together and reaches them out as though he wants to take the two men by the hand and lead them into the other room. Refusing to take his hand, they follow him in to where the body is laid flat and naked on the stone table. The room stinks far more of alcohol now; Andersen has been methodical in his cleaning.

"Look, if you want, but don't touch. The hair, look at the hair."

Joseph leans forward and gazes at the woman's hair, combed back away from the bruised forehead. It is dry now, stiffened with salt or other chemicals. There is nothing particularly notable about it, he thinks. Short-cut, smoothed back from a face that has grown younger and more relaxed in death. The pathologist walks round the body, behind the two men, smiling to himself like a child who's keeping a secret.

"Can't you see it?" Andersen asks.

The three stand there together for some moments in silence before J. D. abruptly snaps.

"Stop talking in riddles, Andersen."

"Ah! I didn't think you'd notice, and you haven't. I looked at her for an hour or two. I thought there was something strange. I wasn't quite sure what, but the bruises didn't make sense. You see, here. If she was hit straight on the brow, like that. The bruise shouldn't curve in that manner, not unless there was something in the way. Something breaking the blow. I wondered what that could be, I looked and I studied and I thought. And then I realised...

"She was wearing something on her head when it

happened. Something that broke the blow a little, altered the shape of the bruise that was made. Something curved, it seemed. And so I did a few little studies. Simple chemistry, textbook stuff. I figured she might have been dressed up, so many people are at the moment. I checked for traces of tin foil. Nada. I'd almost given up. But then I did another test. I gave her hair a wash. There was the usual dirt there, some cigarette smoke. But there was also something else, all mixed in with the sweat and the junk and the rubbish of city life. And then I realised what had softened the blow.

"She looks so regal lying there, doesn't she? I should have realised before." He looks up at J. D. and then at Joseph, then down at the body one more time. "I should have guessed it. When she died, or at least when she was given the blow that killed her, she was wearing a crown. Not just any old tin-foil rubbish, believe me. I've done the tests. Chemical symbol, Ag. This little sweetheart was wearing a crown of nothing less than silver, pure and simple."

The second body in so many days is washed up in much the same place. The man who found the first has taken the day off work. He has pleaded trauma and now he is partying with friends in the corner of a bar, reinventing the story and making himself the hero, looking for sympathy. He is a handsome man and knows how to win sympathy, and he won't be going home alone tonight. This second body is found first by a stray dog, the sort of stray who makes a living out of the sympathy of rich women and the kindness of beggars. It is nuzzling the shoreline in the hope of finding scraps thrown from a barge when it finds the corpse. When it finds the body it begins to howl, and while in fact it is howling in delight – convinced it has found some new and bountiful supply of food – the fact that it is howling will go down on the records in the press as showing the tenderness of animals. *Stray mourns the dead*, the headline tomorrow will read in the high-class paper. *Stray of the Dead*, in the gutter press. And this time, in both cases, it will be a headline, not some obscure back-page note. People always find something thrilling in order, and the similarity between the two bodies is remarkable.

The howling quickly attracts the attention of a group nearby. They are foreign women, mainly, brought in because they are cheap to employ and enjoying their day of freedom. They are cleaners and are dressed in their best clothes, dolled up as maids with powdered faces and rouged cheeks that hide the pallor of their faces when they realised what they've found. Practical women who are used to dealing with unpleasant situations, they haul the body up onto the bank before they call for help. The police come soon and take the body away before the press can take any photographs. By the time it arrives at the station, brought in by four men dragged away from partying, it is four in the morning. Andersen has gone home to his dull little room in the suburbs, stinking of alcohol, and J. D. and Joseph are in the last stages of exhaustion. They don't say much when they see the body brought in, but J. D. quickly does the tests himself and finds the traces of silver dust in her hair. There are no bruises here. It could almost be suicide, if you just looked at her face. But her arms are taped firmly across her body, and underneath them is a clump of paper, wrapped methodically in foil but mortally damaged by water.

With the quick carelessness of someone who is working when almost asleep, J. D. takes the paper and spreads it out. Although once more most of the words are unreadable, the pattern of the words is more evident this time. They are written in ink with a fountain-pen, black words on white paper a little yellowed with age. The name of the woman is actually written in five places in this prayer — but in all of those places the words are quite unreadable. It is only by a happy chance that a few other words are still legible, protected from the worst onslaught of the river-water by the way the girl's hands were folded and taped.

"... *River protect ... Rise and Save ... Water ... Sun and Hope*"

Water, sun and hope.

Seeing the second body disturbs Joseph a little. Because he knew Celice so slightly, this dark-haired woman seems to declare a second death for her and he does not want to go home. He is pleased to accept when J. D. tells him he can share his office if he wants to get some sleep. By five in the morning, the two of them are bedded down on the floor of the office, surrounded by yellowing newspaper clippings which praise the ceaseless virtues of the police.

When you live in a city you grow disrespectful of animals in one way, but also treat them with more reverence in another. With the exception of mice, pigeons and gulls, other small birds and pets, they become something seldom seen. Farmyard beasts are seen as strips of flesh; pigs hang salted in butchers' shops; horses are a novelty for tourists, walking up and down the dry streets, moving higher up in winter or paddling through the shallow waters of the lower squares to save the soles of travellers. This next day, a Tuesday, is a day to acknowledge the animals that have served the city of Galata across the centuries, and the people do so with all the awkward respect and contempt that the majority feel for the creatures they seldom see. For today, they are wearing costumes of animals, all sorts and every kind. And so, when Joseph and J. D. wake to a bright day and step outside, the first thing they see in the late morning air is a march of men and women turned to birds.

It is easy to make a quick costume, if you wish to turn yourself into a bird. You need only feathers, taken maybe from a pillow or a duvet stuffed with the coverings of geese. These costumes have been made fast, in the main. Little children walk along in sneezing awe, their winter coats stitched with white or brown. Chicken feathers, duck feathers, the remnants of Christmas birds. The second body has no name. She looks foreign and serene. Joseph is glad to leave the building and get out amongst the birds.

After a short time walking alongside J. D., Joseph asks to go off on his own. Without saying so, both of them have

accepted him as someone working on this case. He arranges to meet his old friend at dusk in Elohim Square, where the firewalking has been. Then he begins his walk through the streets, thinking about the bodies of one hundred years ago and thinking about the bodies of the animals. He has seen costumes made from animals before, leather jackets or skirts, once or twice a dress threaded through with peacock feathers. This is a different business entirely. Different groups are dressed as different creatures. Joseph is disappointed to find, when he catches an almost-empty barge, that it is filled at the last moment with men dressed as swine, wrapped in the skins of pigs. There is something disgusting about it. The pigskin is too pale, uncured and unprepared. It is like seeing humans wrapped in the skin of other humans. He tries not to breathe in too deeply and he focuses upon the sour leafless trees that overhang the waters.

Joseph is following the first rule of a good detective. If you have no leads to follow, then don't make them. If you have nowhere to go, then go everywhere. He has bought a day ticket for the barges and now he goes up and down the canals. At certain stops, figures dressed as different animals get off and on. Apart from the littlest children, so small that they don't feel afraid, he is the only person dressed in regular clothing. For the first time in a long time, he is struck by how great a presence animals always have in the city. Their flesh. The beating of wings. The statues of imagined animals, the gryphons and the two stone sphinxes that stand on either side of the gates of the city library. Later, most of these animal skins will be burnt, and that will be something to see. For now, the library would perhaps be a good place to go, he thinks. There will be few people there, just words and mainly silence, although the old books of course will be bound with animal skin. He will be able to read the papers for free, to catch up on the news.

The librarian likes to think of himself as a priest among books, and it would please him greatly to think of his books

as taking part in the ceremonies, simply by being leather-bound and silent. He sometimes thinks of the oldest books as ancient prayers. They are held tight and closed, and in the store-room where few people ever go they are fixed almost upright in silver clasps, like palms pointed upward in prayer. And he knows that if you open these books, the most wonderful prayers can come out. You would think they would be filled with darkness from being closed so long. In fact, it is like letting light out into the world, every time.

It took him years to get this far. He seldom has contact with the public now. The library is divided into two parts, very distinctly, as the city is divided into two parts. Outside is the general library, the place to which Joseph will go; the only place he can go without a pass that very few people ever request and far fewer are ever allowed. The librarian served there for years, reading discreetly when he could, showing the quiet deferential calm that marked him for promotion. Now, as the one in charge, he doesn't have much contact with the public and the long struggle all seems worthwhile at last. He kept the murders of his superiors carefully apart. They died years away from each other, in circumstances nobody would have thought mysterious, even if anyone had thought at all. But librarians are solitary creatures in the main, and they had few people if any to mourn them when they were gone. They were married to the books and to their work.

Thirty one years he has worked in the library. Apprenticed at nineteen. But all his life, the whole half-century, the librarian has been haunted by questions in his head. Why do the rivers rise? Why must such a beautiful city die? Sphinxes ask riddles, and libraries are the place to solve riddles but also the only place where the questions are asked. Now he is away from the marches but showing his own form of respect by walking up and down the room stroking the ancient books, whispering church Latin to himself. He can, of course, read silently and when he worked as an assistant in the main library he would always demand that any visitor read their book without speaking.

Latin is different, though, he thinks. It demands to be spoken, it commands the mind and the voice and leaves you with no choice at all.

'Mea culpa, mea culpa, mea maxima culpa. Lord have mercy on us, Christ have mercy on us, Lord have mercy on us.'

The priests have got it all wrong.

He is glad for the silver that clasps the books. It seems wrong to touch them, particularly to touch this volume, the one that has so many answers. He grasps it only by the silver clasps and pulls it open, still tilted upward. He knows the words by heart but it is always better to see them. It is an illustrated book from the fourteenth century, and the golden serpents and dragons that dance against the lettering make seeing a far more spiritual experience than simply remembering. 'Meet brine with blood', he reads the Latin words and smiles. 'Meet water with the moon.' He reads the words out loud to himself, then silently he copies out the crucial prayer over and over, on seven different sheets of old paper. He translates the words from the Latin as he writes, but keeps the meaning the same as far as possible. The meaning, after all, cannot be improved upon. There was one saint who visited the city before saint Mattheus, he thinks. She knew how to hold back the sea, and at the last she gave herself to the sea.

When the librarian has finished writing out the prayer, he takes the seven sheets of thick paper, yellowed with age but still magnificent, and he ties them with string. The woman that he has chosen for tonight is not beautiful but there is a beauty in her eyes that makes her a more than respectable bride for the ocean. For once, the one chosen will not be an artist. It does not seem right for tonight, although he has been surprised at how willing these artistic types have been to offer themselves to the cause. All he had to do was gather them together, show them some of the wonders of the city. Offer to open the ancient books, reveal the beauty of the illustrations. Walk the city at night by firelight, showing where the brine was rising. Young women of a certain age like to feel holy; it makes them feel secure. The group

needed somewhere to belong, and he has certainly provided that. None of them need ever feel again as though they don't belong.

One of the many nice things about the group is that they have money. The woman he has chosen for tonight does not have money and she does not have knowledge, which is what makes her ideal. She simply has the blind animal obedience he requires, and she will walk to the slaughter without even knowing where she is going. He is excited at the thought of it. The calm way in which she will come to the meeting hall, attracted by the idea of money and the sudden friendship she has found amongst the rich. The sudden fear that will bite into her. The slice of the knife on her wrists if she resists and the burning of the words and the way the girl will float upon the waves. Calmly, he takes the writings and binds them in red string and hides them underneath the dark robe that shows his role as the keeper of the books. He walks out of the room then, closing the steel doors to seal the old books in. The doors are strong and only he knows the six digit code that keeps them firmly shut.

As he leaves the outer library he nods goodbye to his assistant. She is a pretty girl, one who could be a friend. Lucia. He wishes she knew, in a way. Perhaps she would understand. She has a look in her eyes, he thinks, that suggests she might. Walking hurriedly past her and out towards the light, he scarcely notices the only visitor to the building today. He only acknowledges him at the last moment, giving a friendly nod as he walks past with his arms folded tightly over the paper. It is always good to be polite, it gets you a long way. Joseph smiles the dry smile of someone quite disinterested. He is reading the news in the papers. The air in the library is dry and his eyes are dry and sore and soon after the librarian has gone he leaves as well. Lucia is left alone then and closes up soon after. Before leaving she presses one hand against the steel of the door that keeps her away from the oldest, most beautiful books. She wishes she could read them. The steel is warm, which is odd in this cool weather, and she thinks perhaps that is because really old books have a life of their own.

It is not a good idea to go walking in the poorer areas, today of all days. J. D. realises this too late. He is a policeman, and so he walks unharmed, but he tries hard not to cause offence and not to notice what animals the people are dressed as. Some, a group of boys, call themselves wolves. But when did you ever see a wolf with spotted fur, J. D. thinks? This is what comes of having the poor area of the city so close to the rich. Both the richest and one of the poorest areas are tight-packed in the old centre; one for the glory, the other for the waste. Boys dressed as dalmatians, pedigree animals that he presumes they stole from somewhere; whooping and laughing and throwing sticks for one another. He should go somewhere else. This isn't a poor man's case, he thinks. The dead girls were rich girls. He doesn't even know what he's doing any more.

Quite soon he leaves the filth and stink of the poor streets and goes to the morgue and sees the two bodies there. Because they both still count as evidence, they have not been touched at all, except by Andersen with his alcohol and his camera-lens. Andersen is not there, nobody is. The room is very cold. He sits down and looks at the girls and he thinks about the writing. After looking at the words on the paper for some time, he is inspired by the ash-frayed edges to go outside and smoke a cigarette. There is a narrow path at the back of the morgue, from which it just looks like a warehouse with particularly harsh lighting. He spits in the water then lights up. The sun is still up, but the moon is starting to rise, chasing it a little although it won't catch up, not yet. When he has finished smoking, he walks through the building and out onto the main street, where he lights another cigarette, laughing at himself for doing so.

J. D. doesn't want to go to Elohim Square again. He just wants to go home and sleep. The idea of all the fake animals disgusts him. It seems a strange way of saying thankyou. But perhaps because he is a policeman, and so always feels he should be where the action is most likely to

occur, he has arranged to meet Joseph there. As he makes his way along he is glad, at least, that he is high ranking enough not to just be on the beat on a night like this. People want to become animals at the best of times. What better way to justify it than by dressing like an animal? Already, as he leaves the morgue and walks through the streets, he sees people growing more aggressive with one another. Their heads are still human but so many of their bodies are wrapped in fur or skin or feathers of some kind. They are shoving each other in the streets. They are forming frightening packs, half human and half animal.

This early on there is still a lot of laughter. But the children, perhaps anticipating the night, are frequently anxious or eager to go home. His own children are maybe crying now, at home. Soon they will pull the curtains closed and switch on the television and watch programmes that have nothing to do with the mad, strange parade of their home city. They will try hard to forget the stink of the uncured skin, or the feathers that swirl in the gutters, blown from old coats by the breeze. But however hard they try to forget, their dreams tonight will be impossible, incredible, and in some way at least, horrific. J. D. remembers nightmares himself. As a child, he was always haunted by nightmares. Still, when he thinks about the children of the city, his own included, he doesn't pity them for their bad dreams. They are at least allowed the time to sleep.

Chapter Four.

The librarian has already chosen the woman he wants for tonight. Anya does not normally work on Tuesdays, but he has paid her half of the money in advance. She has no family and she has nowhere to go, no ties here apart from money. But the fact about those who have no other ties is that money becomes so much, and she must send the money back to her family. He remembers the first time he paid for her. She had not been used to it then. Nervously, she had turned all the photographs on her dresser around. Her family had sent her away to earn money, but she didn't want her father to see how it was earned.

He had slept with her once, of course. It seemed the right thing to do. It put her at ease, it made them comfortable with one another. Then he had left her alone with promises.

"Peter," she says when she meets him at the door. From her mouth it sounds like pieta. He smiles and gives her the money straight away and leads her out into the street. She has made herself pretty for him. She is wearing a white dress and flowers in her hair, just as he asked; cheap flowers, but blue and beautiful. He takes her arm and leads her. To most people watching, they could just be any couple walking through the dusk. Only if you looked very carefully could you see that she doesn't know where she is going; she is being guided. Perhaps Peter is stronger than he looks, because he leads her in the way a father leads a child. They get on a barge with the cattle and the swine. Soon they arrive at the old church, lapped by the waters.

It is so sad, when a place of worship has to be abandoned, and that is what has happened here. The church is no longer a place of worship. The waters are eating it up; rotting the pews and corrupting the walls and desecrating the paintings inside. The silver candlesticks and the altar were removed years ago, along with tapestries and the

congregation. The street that it served has also been abandoned. The foundations of the buildings are foundering and were declared unsafe a decade ago. Without people to offer worship everything goes, even without the degrading influence of the sea.

From outside, the church looks like nothing much. There is no light shining through the windows. Anya, who has grown used to following people for money, nonetheless feels frightened here. She was told that she was going to a party. Perhaps she thought she knew what kind of party this pale man meant. There seems to be nothing here, though. Peter unlocks the door and they walk inside, and into the old church – a meeting hall, now. Above the high water line, reproductions of ancient texts have been fixed into the plaster by metal pins. They sag a little with the moisture in the air.

Leaving Anya standing in the doorway, the librarian walks around the room, lighting candles that stand upright. There are no candle-holders but these candles have been wedged between old books that sit in great heaps around the edges of the room. When he is done he takes off his red gown, which he has worn so proudly all through the streets, and beckons Anya into the room. The sides of the old church have nothing but candles and these old books, dull paperbacks and out-of-date textbooks, science books setting forth their venerable but dated words. The room itself, though, is still made out like a church. There are pews, rotted at the hems and base, water-damaged and stained to half-way up their backs with damp. The stained glass window at the front, which overlooks the canal, is a picture that could be of Mary but that was plainly inspired by the Renaissance, by the classical world. In it, Mary is dressed in blue, beautiful and holy. But she is rising from the waves, like Aphrodite reborn. At once a virgin, and a whore made a virgin once again, Peter thinks. Like Anya was, and like the girl will be again, God willing.

"Make yourself comfortable," he says with the cursory dismissiveness of someone used to treating people like books. "Sit down. I've paid enough, goodness knows. Sit down."

Anya sits, looking around her. She was promised a party; rich people. People like the person she wants to be, Peter said. But it is not seven yet, he tells her. They have half an hour. The people are coming. He just wants some time with her alone before the fun begins.

She sits in the front pew, looking up at the image of Mary rising from the waters. She thinks about her family, the education she is earning for her brother. She imagines to herself that God has sent her this man, a man who will give her the money she needs in exchange for nothing much. She is doing nothing wrong, she thinks. We all need love; Jesus gave his life for love. When all the candles are lit, Peter places the bound papers down underneath the window. There is no light shining through the window now; the image shows from reflected light, candlelight. After a moment gazing at the dark image, he comes and sits beside her. At first he takes her hand like a child, tentative and almost shy. After a moment, however, his other hand reaches up and touches her face. His blue eyes look at her brown eyes, her expression so calm that she must be afraid. Soon he lets go of her hand and slowly unbuttons her white dress, stroking first one breast and then the other. He lowers his head, kissing her lips, then her neck and then her breasts with the tenderest of kisses. His dark hair is grey at the sides, dry and thin as he presses his cheek against her chest. He can hear the heartbeat echoing inside her, the brine of her blood and the movement of her breath. She holds him close, cradling him as much as she can. After a time he asks her to sing, and she sings in her own language, soft songs used normally to lull a child to sleep. He is almost asleep when the time comes, but not so drowsy that he doesn't hear the footsteps of the first of his helpers walking up the steps outside. Quickly he sits up and gestures to Anya, who buttons up her dress. The doorlatch clicks, and the first of them is inside.

Rebecca is wearing a dress of blue and carrying a purse of money, mainly stolen from her parents. She is seventeen and plain, mesmerised by the books the librarian has shown her. She walks up the aisle and sits down beside him,

looking at the prostitute who is gazing blankly at her with an expression that is trying to pull back some dignity. Soon Daniel comes too, a fair-haired man who was charmed from the first by what the librarian said. The claim that with a little blood, we can hold back the sea. The last man, who chooses to be known as John, was the one who told the good news to the others. His personality is a happy combination, one that proved perfect to the librarian. He is strong willed but gullible; he will believe what he is told quite readily, but once he has been told he can convince others with a forceful charm that the librarian has never had. Swiftly, the librarian moves forward and kisses him once on one hand, once on the other. They love each other, as one God must love another if he only dares to recognise him.

It is amazing what money can do. Anya is still quite calm, even now, thinking of the money she will be able to send home. People with so much money must be trusted; they must be kind; otherwise, why would God have granted them so much? She is thinking this right up to the moment when John takes her hands. He kisses both, and despite herself she wonders with excitement at what it would be to love him. She is wondering this right up to the moment when, with one swift movement, he takes both hands and twists her wrists and holds them behind her back. Perhaps part of her is still wondering as her arms are tied by the librarian, in schoolboy knots that are simple but secure. The librarian asks her to be calm. They mean only to love her, only to give her gifts. Smiling but talking too quickly for comfort, he reads the prayer in Latin. She does not understand much Latin, but perhaps she catches the word for blood, sanguine, the way that the librarian's tongue seems to love that word. Perhaps that is what makes her struggle and makes her start to scream. Calmly, John takes some silver tape and tapes her scared lips closed. The other woman watches on in wonder. She is proud, to think that another of her sex will give her life to hold back the sea.

After the prayer is read in Latin, it is read once more in the vernacular. Anya cannot move, although she will not

stop trying. The others do not hurt her, though. They merely hold her down. The ocean is rising outside. The canal is lapping against the wall, as the two men force the young girl forwards – as she is made to climb the three steps up towards the window. It is John, alone, who pulls back the girl's hair to reveal her face. She looks around her, the candlelights reflected in her eyes. She closes her eyes at the very end, but that does not mean she doesn't feel the knife.

☩

By the time Joseph arrives at Elohim Square, the dark has truly set in and people are making pyres of animal skins. There are three separate bonfires, unlit at the moment, all stinking of fur and feathers. As he stands there, more and more people come into the square and take off their costumes and throw them on. There are no children there, but childrens' costumes come too, carried by mothers or fathers. One pyre for the men, another for the women, another for the children. The whole idea just copies what was done one hundred years ago, then a hundred years before that, back into the past. They are just trying to hold back the sea. Nobody there really believes in what they are doing. But with the moon far more than half full and rising above the square, it is easy to imagine they are in another time, even when they bring out the cans of petrol and spew it over the pyres. It is easy to conceive that making sacrifices like this, showing their gratitude to the sea and to God, might just help to hold back the waves.

By the time J. D. arrives the sea is as high as it will get, and lapping through the thin streets nearest to the canal. It is shallow enough here that it only moistens the soles of his shoes, and thankfully it has not quite reached Elohim square yet. That will happen in a couple of days, at full moon. He walks into the square and looks around him at the men and women, now dressed normally in the main; the young men sometimes topless to show off their muscles, but flexing those muscles to ward away shivering. Soon he sees Joseph and makes his way towards him.

55

"You made it on time," Joseph says as he approaches. J. D. smiles and nods, saying nothing. He has spent the day searching the streets, and he has found nothing to speak about. All he has seen have been people walking, getting more wild as time has gone on, getting more furious. He, too, is furious now. He stands beside Joseph and frowns as people add more and more skins to the mounds before them.

They stand there for almost an hour, drinking beer that they buy from one of the stalls that line the square. It is cheap and unpleasant and weak. Most of the people there are drinking strong cider, and the stink of petrol is combined with the rotten-sweet smell of apples and alcohol. At nine, six men still dressed as cattle come and stand outside the temple, in front of the pyres. They dance then, an abrupt dance that is half taken from very old books, half inspired by drink. At the very end, all of the men throw off their skins and place them on the pyre. Then one steps forward. He is very tall and young, a handsome man holding a flaming torch in one hand. Carefully, he lights the pyres one by one. The flames flicker awkwardly, then surge up towards the sky. The people clap then and dance together. The older figures are fully dressed, in suits or weekend clothes, smart but casual. Many of the younger men and women are almost naked; beautiful bodies moving forwards against the flame. From time to time, a burning feather catches the wind and whirls out against the cobblestones.

J. D. looks out at the young men and women in the square and thinks about what he was taught at school. This is tradition, and therefore sacred. They must make these sacrifices and these processions through the week, just to give thanks for the fact that such a great city is still alive. But the fact is that the city is dying. More than that. People are dying. Apart from the brief brittle excitement of reading it in the news, though, nobody seems particularly to care. The figures before him and Joseph are laughing, dancing, delighting in the fact that law has fallen away. The policemen that stand in the square are unsure what to do; uncertain how far tradition can be said to hold sway, or at

what point they should step in. They are very few against
the crowd, and their fingers press nervously against their
guns. What would happen if the people got angry, they
wonder? What would they do? How would the people
react, now, if a bullet was fired into the group?

✝

Lucia is also standing in the square. She is young, and many
people would call her beautiful, but while she has her fair
share of men trying to coax her into the dance she stays in
the shadows with her hair hung low against her face. She
remembers what she learned at school herself. Like so many
young people, she does not believe in anything much but
she wishes passionately that she could. She remembers
being taught about the great marches of the past. A good
student, she can even remember what Spencer Manville
wrote about the great marches that marked the five
hundredth anniversary of the city.

I have seen nothing to stir the blood, the scholar and
merchant reflected, *so much as the common masses when they
pull together to give thanks to God. Truly, we are all as
sovereigns in the kingdom of Heaven.*

It makes her laugh a little to think about it. The notion
that we are all kings, written down by the richest man of his
time. The richest man, in real terms, of all time in the city.
It must have been easy for him to believe. For herself, she
will be grateful for tomorrow. The fourth day, written
down as a day of rest all those centuries ago; a day of
recovery after the desperate sacrifices of the first holy
weekend. It is after tomorrow that the true, awe-filled
sacrifices must begin. She remembers reading about the
weekend that will follow in books, as a child. The books
were edited and scientific, like sex education texts that only
lay down facts and give nothing away about emotions. Still,
the words were wonderful, with the kind of taut wonder
and nervousness that she imagines the earth must hold
immediately prior to some great destructive tremor.

Lucia stands and looks at the burning animal skins,

preferring the dancing of the flames to any other dance that she might watch. The people here don't matter, she thinks. It is tradition that matters, and tradition is stronger than all of the people here. Tradition is something that surges and recedes, like the tide; that presses and then falls away, and yet is always there. She loved to read those stories about the sacrifices made by the people, at the end of every century. It has always been a holy struggle to hold back the sea. Staring at the flames, the young girl smiles to think of where she is now; working at the library, surrounded by books, steeped in history. Tomorrow she will go to work, and she will read about the ancient traditions that are being repeated here and now. She will think about the past and the present, and it will make her proud to be part of something greater than the trivial everyday concerns of all the world. There was something that Peter said today, she thinks, that it is important to remember. To predict the future, he told her, we need only look back at the past. She remembers how when she was young, she was always fascinated by the past.

The fires are not dying down by the time that Lucia leaves, at eleven. They are still alive at one, when Joseph and J. D. leave, each of them going now to his own home for the first time in days, grateful for the day of rest that will follow. But while they are still burning strong, they are no longer blazing. Theirs is another sort of flame now; a deep flame. The outside fires have flickered away, but deep within the skins at the very heart of every pyre are only just twisting into life, turning life into ashes. They are sparked into awareness by the petrol that is doused over, and over, and over again. The young will stay here until dawn at least, forcing flame after flame from dead skin.

Normally Joseph would be woken by his radio alarm at eleven AM. It is a failsafe, a safeguard against the possibility that he might sleep far too late. Day after day he has lain awake listening to the local radio playing classic favourites dedicated to people in cafes and garages and offices, feeling

the pain of the old wound, wondering at the pins and iron that hold the bone together. There has been no reason for him to wake up for years, and that is why he needs the radio. Otherwise he sleeps until afternoon, then needs to drink to find sleep again before dawn.

Today, as always, the radio clicks on at eleven, but for once Joseph is awake to hear it. He is awake to hear the sudden slight switch, the shift to on. He is awake, but too drowsy for a moment to understand why all he hears from the radio, at that instant when it stirs into life, is silence. Not static, and not the silence of an unpowered machine. This is different, a state-sponsored silence. As he shakes the weariness from his mind he remembers why. Every city radio station will be silent today. National television will continue, national radio, but the spaces set for local news will be blank. Everything, everywhere, in the media that might suggest that life in the city continues will be blank. Today is the day of silence, the fourth day. Today is the day of rest. Tabula Rasa.

Clapping his hands, Joseph gets out of bed and walks to the window. He opens the shutters and looks out. Outside people are walking up and down, uncertain of quite what to do. Birds are singing but people are mainly voiceless, hungover. There are two children down below, sketching a game in the pavement with chalk. Joseph moves to pick up the phone, dials a number quickly, and talks to J. D.'s wife when she answers.

"Cass. Yes, Joseph. Long time."

Long time.

"Look, can I talk to John?"

John Douglas is playing with his youngest son, who has just discovered he can make a gun with the fingers of his hand. He is pretending to die when Joseph calls; an overdramatised death, one from television or film, a cackling kind of tragedy. He tries to persuade Joseph to come over and meet him at his house, but Joseph says no. He doesn't want to see Cass again. He doesn't want to see the children that she and J. D. have together, their neat little life. He prefers to think all the police are like him; he

prefers not to be reminded of what he does not have. Fairly quickly the two arrange to meet in a café and soon after that Joseph dresses and leaves the flat, walking down the stairs two at a time. It is a sunny day, the sort of day that encourages things like that.

At first glance, the city today seems completely normal. The flaming torches have been swept away; the street cleaners have been busy, brushing the sacrificed hours and animals into nothing. But the difference about today is more disturbing for its subtlety. Joseph knew what was coming, alongside everyone in the city, but that does not mean he likes it. He is a man who thrives on news, who wants to know everything. That, as much as the prestige and the violence, was why he joined the police. Today, everything is blank.

He sees it when he walks past the newsagent, and although he laughs it is a nervous laugh. The city has embraced this day of enforced emptiness to a ridiculous degree. There are no national broadsheets or tabloids in the stands. The only newspapers that are allowed here are local ones, and only the blind could call them newspapers. Because underneath the familiar bannerheads of the city's press, there is no news at all. It is absurd to see, or would be if the idea behind it were not so serious. There are three main papers in the city, and all of them are for sale. All of them contain the same number of pages as always; all are headed in the same way as they are every day. But underneath the bannerheads there is nothing but emptiness. Sheet after sheet of plain, cheap paper, folded over.

When he arrives at the café J. D. is already sitting there. The clouds are gathering and it is starting to spit; nonetheless, he sits outside, alongside others who are trying to persuade themselves the water is still gentle. Although he is dressed plainly there is something about his expression and manner that make him seem different from the others there. For one, he is the only person there who has not bought a newspaper. The rest of the customers are drinking their coffees with their heads bent over blank pages. J. D. sits there alone, looking into space, his thin face tired and

reflective. Joseph knows the idea behind today. He has read his history. Today is supposed to be a day of rest not just in the middle of the festival. It is also meant to be a day of rest after the century that has passed; a day to contemplate a hundred years of history. In order to truly think about history, the idea runs, one must inhabit a day in which history is not really happening.

The two drink coffee and eat cheap biscuits and gaze at the shadows from the plane trees above. Their coffees are espresso and they drink them slowly, swilling the dark strength around their teeth, letting it burn their gums. They hardly talk at all, at first, except to order more drinks.

"You look half asleep," Joseph says in the end.

"I've been thinking about history," J. D. replies.

Joseph laughs at this.

"You and the rest of the city."

"True. But look. Today's *supposed* to be a day for considering the past. I've been thinking about those girls. The way they went into the water."

J. D. grimaces, taking in the grit at the base of his coffee, and orders another. Inside the café a canary in a cage is singing, or at times losing its song and picking at its feathers in bland bemusement.

"Look," he says. "I don't have *any* leads on this. But one thing I know, is that whoever's killing these girls knows too much about the past. This is not just some copycat who's bought a book and worked their thoughts up into fury about it. The murders are too precise for that."

"How do you mean?"

"Well, it's like this. A few people like history. A few people read books. Quite a few people read books about murder, don't they? So I thought to myself, whoever's doing this has bought themselves a book about the past. They get the idea of girls floating in the rivers, it flicks a switch, they do it themselves. Case open – though not shut, because we can't guess who it is. But I looked on through my library last night, Joseph. People know about the murders a hundred years ago. But there are some 'details' the police never let out."

"Like?"

"Well… Take silver crowns for example. No one ever said about the silver crown. It's too close to what's sacred. The public should never know the truth about religion, you must know that. And nowhere – *nowhere* – does any book say a single word about the fact that the last girl, unnamed, was found wearing a silver crown. Or take…"

"The papers?"

"Right. There's nothing about them anywhere. I told you about the few words we have. From the girls a hundred years ago, 'Water … Sun and Hope'. None of it ever entered the press. None of it ever made its way into any book about the murders. None of it is known to anyone."

Joseph isn't surprised at this. The police keep everything back.

"Well…" J. D. shrugs. "I thought about that. Those words came up again, this week. And this time there was more. 'River Protect … Rise and Save … Water, Sun and Hope'. Sounds like a prayer, doesn't it? So I searched through the bible, looked at prayer books. I was about to give up. But then this morning, after I spoke to you, I had an idea. Nowadays, people pray in their own language, don't they? But a hundred years ago, they prayed in Latin."

Carefully, he bends down under the table and reaches into a leather holdall. He pulls out one sheet of printed paper and hands it to Joseph as though it were old and sacred.

"You won't find this in any prayer-book, but believe me it *is* a prayer."

Joseph picks up the paper and looks at it carefully. Today is, after all, a day for considering history. He looks at the words, and he tries to make sense of them. It's been such a long time since he had to read Latin.

✝

It takes half an hour to travel all through the city on the great river, a journey that guidebooks generally promote as being one of the greatest in the world. Perhaps it is not that,

but there is something about it that inevitably stimulates an emotion deep in the gut of the uninitiated, and continues to fire up the librarian every time he makes the journey. Perhaps it is the purposelessness of it. Very few people ride the whole way for a reason, and sitting here is a wonderful way to spend a day that you are trying to pretend does not exist. Not many people have realised this, the librarian thinks, but it's true. He is dressed normally now. The dark blood under his fingernails has oxidised fully and looks like everyday city grime. He keeps his fingernails clipped short to protect the books, but it is impossible to keep them cut so close that he can fully keep out the dirt.

Perhaps, he thinks, it is the proportions of the buildings on either side that creates an unsettling feeling. The Renaissance began hundreds of miles away in another, distant country, and trickled here at first in a few books and in the mind of one or two bewildered foreign travellers. The great ancient buildings are majestic now, but when they were built they already seemed dated to those who journeyed from the south. They were forced up at the end of the neo-classical period, when classic architecture was dying from the base up. Traditional in the main, the buildings are nonetheless unsettled by twists of the baroque; the general impression must from the start have been one of an old man trying to keep up with the times.

The library is open today. Lucia has opened the doors and even now she is sitting behind the desk. Now and then people walk in, just to look at the novelty of the empty papers. But the librarian is not working. He is just travelling, looking at the way that clouded light cripples itself on the water, waving away into nothingness. The river is too wide for the buildings on either side, he is thinking. Their shadows could not possibly stretch across. As he makes the journey, he looks in part at these buildings, but most of his attention is paid to the people who get on and off the river-bus, paying their fares and travelling a little way and getting on with this empty day. There are more passengers now, sheltered under the roof, with the rain coming in from the sea. He watches them all.

When you only make a short journey you do not realise how many people there are. They get on and off, their faces change. They hardly ever look out at the world. Old men hang their heads and snooze in the rain, sheltered slightly by the roof of the river-bus but unshielded from the wind that blows drizzle in from the sides. Young men and women ignore one another. Sometimes it seems to the librarian that he is the only person who notices anyone. He notices everything. He imagines the names of the people, their lives. They are all God's children and they are all beautiful. Every now and then they move under a bridge. Aisha bridge, a concrete arch built in the seventeen hundreds, a perfect pure span spoiled by unnecessary curlicues. The rusting iron of Oerim bridge, salt-damaged, paint-stripped, naked in the rain. This is where the divers come in summer, risking their lives to impress women, throwing themselves into the water and swimming to the edge.

He remembers doing it himself.

That had been a beautiful year. The sun had seemed to shine every day. He had made his way to the iron bridge most days, and stood at the edge looking out. Then one day, in mid-summer, something had told him to do it. He had seen other people do it and it had not seemed hard. And so he had waited, watching for a space in the river's traffic, and when it had come he had thrown himself off the bridge and into the water.

As the river-bus travels underneath the iron bridge now, the librarian remembers the shatter of the water around him when he dived. The thrill of swimming deeper, trying to find the darkness. Determined to reach the depths. He had swum with all his strength, holding his breath until his muscles ached, desperate and elated. And so he had touched the bottom, just once. Scraped the mud with his fingers, reached right into the heart of the river. It had been one of the greatest moments of his life. He had reached deep into the heart of something, and he had come out alive. But he had been younger then, and stronger, and he doubts that he could do so now.

Chapter Five.

By the time the librarian has travelled all the way to the stop closest to the sea, it is well past midday. He is hungry and he likes this because it makes him feel more alert. The clouds against the sea are darkening more now and he rides back with them, feeling the promise of storm chase him as he sits on the returning boat. He has not always been called Peter; it is a name he took, the only name he likes to have now. On certificates and contracts, his name is something different. But he has willed himself so fully to forget his past that he has really become quite good at it, and he seldom thinks on this. The name he was given by his parents, after all, was never really his.

The blank slate day.

He smiles.

Most of the time, he can't even remember his own last name.

Peter sticks his palms out of the side of the barge, one after the other, and gathers in the water that is falling. He wishes it were clean, but he knows that even rainclouds here are dusty with the dirt of the city; dead skin, dead factories, dead days. He thinks about it for a long time and he presses his face out against the rain. Perhaps the people around him think that he is strange for doing this, but they would think him stranger still if they could see the tears he is crying for them.

Strangers are always uncomfortable with the love that Peter feels.

When he has journeyed all the way back into the heart of the city, he gets off the boat and walks along the side of the river. After a while he turns and makes his way along one of the small roads. He is in the foreign quarter now, but he is pleased to see that even the small papers published by foreigners have respected the tradition of the day. The newspapers are kept in stands outside, and although they

are under shelter the rain is blowing inward now and spattering across their sheets. The rain is making the cheap ink of the headlines run. Their dark banners are streaking downward. The vast empty space beneath the titles is stained with greyblack lines where the water has trickled downward.

Soon the blankness will be unreadable.

The librarian has come into the foreign section of the city because he knows how the people are here. Many of them do not even speak the language well. Most of them diligently find jobs in the service industry; bowing their heads, pursuing the dream. But others are violent, and some are desperate, and it is possible to buy almost anything here if you know the right people.

The man he is about to meet is known as Ezekiel, but that is only because he is very old and the name amuses the people who know him; mainly people from other countries, who find the streetnames of the city strange and play with the idea of them in order to blend in. He runs a pawn shop where you can buy and sell pretty much anything, although he does not deal with technology because that makes him uncomfortable. Still you can trade wrist-watches there and silver plate and foreign antiques and hand-me-downs. Some young women have even been known to sell their hair, cutting it off with brisk regret. He sells this on to wig-makers, because there is always a market in hair, particularly the blonde-gold hair of foreign girls.

When the bell rings in the shop Ezekiel walks out slowly from the backroom. He walks like a beetle would walk if it were made human; with a scuttling hunch. His hair, too, was once yellow but now it is grey and clipped short. He smiles when he sees the librarian, and leads him into the backroom, which he locks promptly. This is the room where he does most of his business. The poor and the lonely sometimes want to dispose of children, and he offers both the best prices and the greatest assurance to desperate mothers.

"It's good to see you," he says, lying to the librarian. "You look good, man."

Ezekiel is wearing a new suit, slightly too baggy for his skinny old body. His lies are like his clothes, Peter thinks. They don't quite fit, but they are elegant and well-made. The backroom is brighter than it used to be, lit by a new and more powerful bulb in a spherical paper shade. On either side of the room are three cribs, but only one of them contains a baby. She is silent. The simple smell of codeine fills the room. Peter has seen Ezekiel tend to children before, rubbing codeine on their gums to make them sleep, feeding them cow's milk or mush. He doesn't want to see it again. Sensing this, perhaps, the old man reaches into the only filled crib, the one furthest from the door. The baby girl is very small, perhaps she was premature. She is sleeping calmly, but Peter likes to think she is dreaming of nothing.

"I saved her for you," he says. "You provide for her a good home?"

"The best." Peter smiles. He knows where the children here normally go. Most are sold to women who are desperate to have children of their own. Rich women, rich families like his own.

"Man," says Ezekiel. "It's hard to believe. Long time. The longest. I held you. I wiped you. People tend to forget about me, you know."

The librarian thinks back to his childhood. If more children were told, he thinks, then they would never forget. He shrugs and reaches into his pocket, pulling out his wallet and then counting out the notes.

"I'm giving you a special rate," says Ezekiel. "You've got to look after your own." His hands are shaking a little as he says this. Perhaps it is the thought of the money; maybe the awareness of everything the librarian knows. It is uncomfortable to share secrets with people you haven't seen for so long, and in truth he can't picture the baby that the man in front of him once was. It has been fifty years.

"This one, she had a beautiful mother. As beautiful as yours, almost."

"My mother's dead."

Peter is sure of this. She would have come for him otherwise.

"Of course. You got rich, though. You got lucky. An only child. You do good by her. You're a good man."

After Peter has handed him the money, Ezekiel gives him the child tenderly. He does not like to think of himself as being a bad person, and he is glad to know that he is handing her on to someone rich, who knows what it is like. She is swaddled carefully, and Peter is pleased to see that even without him asking Ezekiel has wrapped her little body in a blue blanket. Blue is the colour of innocence and of the sea. As he looks down at her he is in many ways glad that she is fast asleep. He tilts his face downwards and kisses her on the forehead. Even in sleep she reacts to him, pursing her lips up as though she is looking for her mother's breast.

Lucia is working alone in the library, even though her work should be finished. It has closed early, because nothing is supposed to be open after dusk today. That is when the power everywhere switches off. There will be no electricity throughout the city now until midnight. It shows the fact that this night does not exist. The power station itself is virtually shut down, almost unmanned. But although it is an evening when everyone is meant to forget, she is busy now, despite the fact it is after five and it has been dark for almost an hour. The weather is bad outside and while she knows it is getting worse, still she does not want to leave. She has candles ready and she has an idea.

For so many months she has thought about it. The steel door, the old books and manuscripts inside. They are always so well protected. Kept from everything, from fire and water and danger. She was able to see them only once. Those ancient words were fascinating; the gold and the ink chasing one another, pressed against the page. Ever since, she has longed to be allowed in there on her own. She has seen the keys so many times, hanging on the hook. But the sirens are so loud.

There was a time, she recalls, when she asked Peter for

the code that would switch off the siren. Peter was never drunk but that one time, her birthday, he had swilled red wine all day, and by the end of the day he had been talking about anniversaries and swearing she was his only friend. He would share the books with her, he would show them all to her. They could be friends together. Lucia had smiled at this, touched by his fondness and – in her childish way – thinking of him as an old man. He had led her in, turning off the code and unlocking the door with the silver key. He had kept her always at a distance. But when he had shown her the books he had chosen to show, the Latin and gold and glass cases, he had locked away the room again and reset the alarm. It had been then that she had asked him for the pass-code, her voice as friendly as she could make it but nervous nonetheless. Peter had shaken his finger at her melodramatically, although she had seen he was laughing at the same time.

"Oh no. That room, that's only for me and God."

He had kissed her once on the forehead, then kissed her on the lips. She had allowed this because of what he had shown her. It had seemed only fair at the time.

Ever since, she has been waiting for this moment.

She has known it since dusk. The moment that the lights flickered, then failed.

Prolonging the excitement, perhaps worried that she would be discovered the moment the power went down, Lucia has spent the last hour cleaning by candlelight. Now, though, she walks to the backroom where the silver key hangs loose and heavy on the curve of a pointed hook. She takes it in one hand, a candle held firmly in the other. The wax dribbles slightly against her skin, but she tries not to notice as she unlocks the door. It opens smoothly and cleanly and, of course, there is no alarm.

A day that is not supposed to really be is necessarily a nightmare for the police. On one hand, they are meant to pretend that they too do not exist; to stay silent and still, to

hide themselves away after dusk. All of the lights in the city are off, and nothing is meant to be happening. But despite the desire of the police to be seen to do nothing, criminals will be eager to make the most out of the stillness of the city. Policemen, then, are standing in groups outside in the streets and watching anyone who walks past. There are no streetlamps and no houselights, and this evening could be violent. They are afraid of looting, of madness. Anyone wandering the streets tonight, when everything should be still, might be a criminal. In many ways, they are glad for the storm even though it means that their job is less comfortable. Only the most desperate thieves would be out in the dark and the rain which is now pouring down everywhere, running in the gutters and streaming down the pipes.

Because of the police on patrol, Joseph and J. D. are forced to present their ID cards over and over again. There are no streetlamps but the police have torches which they flash very readily in the faces of anyone they see. It becomes tiresome very quickly. The clothes of the two men are soaked but they have made an oath to do what they have to do. Having read the prayer and translated it clumsily, they still have very few leads but they know one truth. They have to search the churches of the city.

This is not difficult to do, because the churches at least are open tonight, although only lit by candlelight. The moment people start to feel emptiness, many of them want to fill their minds with thoughts of God. The pair realise this as soon as they reach the cathedral in the main square, each of them cradling a torch. After the bright giddiness of last night, the empty silence of the open space is particularly unsettling. There are no sounds there except for the sounds of the storm. But they can see straight away that the candles in the cathedral are on, and its doors unlocked, though closed.

The rain is pouring down and there are flashes of light out to sea, although it is not yet possible to see lightning as streaks of electricity. At the moment it shows as nothing more than little flares of white fire that seem to fill the

clouds for a moment then fall away. As they walk into the building Joseph flashes his torchlight upward and sees the statues of angels high above them. They are massive and he remembers being told as a child that these statues were carved carefully, with grooves cut in their faces for the tears to run down, tears which only come when it rains. The doors open easily. Inside the cathedral is filled with people. None of them are singing and none of them are speaking. They just sit there, strangers together, trying hard to think about nothing but haunted by the thoughts of storm and candlelight.

After they have finished in the cathedral Joseph and J. D. discuss where to go next. Because it is so dark J. D. finds himself talking in a whisper. There are so many churches left to see.

"You take the left of the river."

Joseph explores every church on the left hand side of the swollen water, watching J. D. cross the bridge before he starts. All are open and all have worshippers tonight by candlelight, if you can call the silent introspection that has overcome the city worship. He walks up and down the streets, feeling the thinness of dark alleyways pressing against his gut, hating the shadows. He sings to himself as he goes, silently. Angry at the state of the city, the absolute night, he tries to flood his mind with memories. It is difficult, with the storm so furious. He remembers his childhood and his training. The pressure in the air is making his body hurt, particularly in the joints and the old wound that scars his skin. His clothes are soaked and he never visits any church for long enough for them to dry. He only looks around, peering at engravings, tilting the light of his torch at Latin carvings next to images of the dead. He searches for hours, trying to recognise more than a few words from the prayer in every prayer he reads. The map he carries shows every active church, marking them with little red crucifixes. He is amazed that there are so many, each one filled with people still praying. But then, he was never a religious man.

Peter cradles the baby so gently underneath his coat. She does not wake for a long time, and when she does finally regain consciousness he is surprised to find her not sobbing but giggling at the rain. It is as though the storm, which even he finds frightening, delights her. Perhaps it is just the last of the drugs in her system, but it pleases him. It is wonderful to own her. A little girl without a name. At one point, there in the rain, he folds open his coat and lets a little water touch her on the brow. He does not give her a name, not yet, but he imagines that the city itself is christening her. He walks through the streets and listens to the storm and thinks on the lightning flashing out to sea. It wants to clean away the city. They never even notice.

He reaches the old church early and goes inside and lights a few candles, as few as are necessary because he doesn't want to be noticed. At seven the others arrive. They stand at the front of the building, surrounded by books. One by one, they hold the child. Every one of them christens her in turn, in his or her own name. Rebecca, Daniel. Peter, John. The girl represents all of them. She is clean, she is empty. She is a new start. After they have christened her they lay her down beside the font. At the side of the pews are bottles of cheap red wine. The quality doesn't matter, it is just meant to represent blood. Quickly they drink together then pray together. Afterwards, Peter takes the seven prayers he has copied for her and lays them down before the stained glass. They have been kept dry and they burn easily. When they have burned, the others leave, glad to have given the baby their names. She will start their lives afresh for them, they have been told. It is a beautiful truth.

"It's time to give her back to her mother."

It's what they want to believe.

When they are gone, Peter holds her for a long time and when she cries he numbs her tears with wine. Blowing all but one of the candles out, he drinks alone. He wonders who her mother was, and he is glad to think that she will

have a new mother soon. He will give her to her mother. She looks so calm and gentle that it would be quite wrong to do otherwise.

It is very near midnight when he and the baby leave the abandoned church. The tide is lapping up near to its abandoned foundations and the river is very easily reachable. As they walk towards it in the dark he sings lullabies to the drunken baby, who is asleep and will not hear them. She is so peaceful that she does not even hear the thunder of the storm, directly overhead. Peter is pleased at how well he has planned everything. A little before twelve, he is standing alone on Aisha bridge, surrounded by nothing but darkness and stone. It is the oldest bridge that still remains, so old that it seems very low above the risen river. He chose it because of the rituals that he has read about, but the fact it is so close to the water is, he thinks, a happy coincidence. It means people seldom use it to cross. It will mean, too, that the baby has less far to fall. He kisses her once on the forehead, partly through love, and then he lets her go.

After she has gone Peter feels clean for the first time in a long time. It is not long before the rivers will start going down now, he knows it. Only one more sacrifice. And then... It is time for the world to make a new start. As if they understand what he is thinking, at midnight precisely all the streetlights around him flare on. Forgotten houselights flicker into being and the city is bright again. The storm seems less with the lights on, but it still feels strong. Because he is allowed to think of history again, Peter does not immediately return home to the house that his parents left him. Instead he walks to the library to think about the books there and what they all mean to him. He is surprised when he arrives to see the electric lights are all on.

Perhaps Lucia forgot to switch them off when she left, he thinks.

Or perhaps she is working late.

As soon as the streetlamps flare on at midnight the preparations begin. Joseph, walking home after searching every living church on his side of the river, sees people already dragging kitchen tables and dining tables out through their front doors. Elsewhere, in the streets of shops, cheap plywood tables have been placed all along the pavement in an awkward row, with the ridges between the tables uneven where the paving beneath is cracked. Children are asleep and, he notices, most of the men are too. Here in the old heart of the city it is women who are preparing most for the following day. With the tired strength of mothers they arrange the tables, carrying them and slotting them into place. The police look on and at times try to flirt with the women, some of whom are dressed in night-clothes and some of whom are still dressed. Today of all days, they think, they might even get lucky with the married ones. The coldness makes the skin on the bodies of women seem fresh and young beneath thin clothes. As they prepare for the feast that is coming with the daylight, Joseph looks at them with sad excitement, walking home alone.

The fifth day, Joseph thinks. Although he is exhausted, and his search has found nothing, still he cannot help feeling a taut ache of exhilaration at the thought. The cleansing has been done now and the lights are all on. The celebration of rebirth can take place. The fifth day, the old writings say, is the day of Man. Conscious of the weight of sexism the title holds, the council have declared its official title to be the day of Galata. No-one is taken in by this title. Today is the day of Man. Today is a day to celebrate the deepest human pleasures. The thought of it makes his head hurt. Inside, Joseph is torn between feeling a part of the city in a way he never has before, and a growing awareness of his own loneliness. He wants to grab one of these women, to beg a kiss from her. If he was younger, perhaps he would have the courage.

J. D., meanwhile, is not feeling lonely as he returns home. He is disappointed at his futile search, and angry at himself, and he needs comfort. He walks in quietly and wakes up his wife by kissing her up and down her back. She is so tired

from preparing the meal for the following day that she stirs unwillingly at first. He, too, is exhausted but both of them know what tonight is all about.

"Fucking first and feasting after," he says. "Come on, come on. We're not too old."

It is not curious that the librarian, too, as he enters the library at that moment is thinking almost exactly the same thing. Today is a day for fucking and feasting; that's what the common folk say, and while he prides himself on not being common he cannot help the words that come into his head. He has never been able to prevent those. And so it is with a brisk thrill of delight that he realises, at first, that Lucia is still in the library. He has seen the way she looks at him when she doesn't think he's watching. The way she watches him, wondering at his maturity, wondering what it would be like to hold an older man. He has teased her about this, although only in his mind. Older men make better lovers. He has said the words to her so many times, in his head, and he is not surprised to think that at last they have reached her. It would have to be today that she realised. It could only be today. It could only be the day of man.

Feeling a sense of dream, as though he were being carried away by the river of his thoughts, Peter does not even realise at first that the door to the inner library is open. He thinks to himself that the young girl must be waiting somewhere in the aisles for him. She could only be waiting for one reason, he thinks. There is only one reason why a pretty girl like her would still be here at this time of night, on this night of all nights. He walks up and down the aisles for some time before he finally notices. The metal door has been pulled closed, and the lights inside are dim to protect the precious manuscripts. But there is the sound of singing from inside, the distracted singing of someone who is busy doing something else. It is not much of a song, he thinks, but it is something and he knows he will ask her to keep singing even while they are making love.

Chapter Six.

Lucia is reading one of the old manuscripts, an illustrated manuscript from the 14th century. Her heart is beating fast as she reads, because she has been told since childhood, alongside everyone else in the city, that this manuscript was lost long ago. Pieces of it are quoted in other books, of course. But the manuscript, she was told, was burned hundreds of years ago. The account of Thomas Burthen, priest. She could not believe it when she first read the words, in a clumsy scrawl on the skin of the manuscript. The truth behind the celebrations, written back when people knew what they really meant. Like all celebrations nowadays, the festival has been trimmed down and hemmed in. The more distasteful aspects have been glossed over. That is the natural way. For hours now, first by candlelight and then by the dim electric lights of the inner library, she has been reading from the original manuscript of the only remaining account of the true festivities. She has been reading words that everyone thought were dead. The descriptions of how to hold back the sea. Much of what is written here is recorded elsewhere. But the manuscript was thought lost long ago.

And some there were who claimed a 2nd flood, a Time of Reckoning, Must Come. For we are all sinners, and does not God declare that Sin must not go Unpunished? And so it is in this Great City, the Greatest of All Cities and the Greatest Place of Sin. And so it is with Us, that Punishment must come. And so did the elders decide, on the first turning of the century, one truth. You who live by the temper of the sea, know that the oceans must be tempered with blood. This is the true chronicle of that which has been known by tongue for centuries.

It was spoken long before it was written, meet brine with blood. This FACT was reckoned thus: that in order to live in Harmony with the Ocean, Man must Give to Receive. For the first century was a time of Fever and the threat of sea and of Man's Brittle Hate, and of enmity with the ocean that was met by Unbidden Death. And many did die of the sickness, and desperation was upon all, and the Ocean took and took again.

And so it was that on the Hundredth year, desperation overtook the city, and death was everywhere and Black Flies ate the dead. This was a time of fear, and it seemed the city would fall into the sea. But as the Sun does follow night, so there arose a mighty Foe of darkness. She did rise up from the slums, and she was a Saint as No Other. For she was a saint of Life and Death, and She was Saint Sophia.

Lucia knows *these* words already. Everyone in the city knows them. They were recorded in a print book soon after they were handwritten, before the papers in front of her disappeared. The words from the print book have been quoted by schoolbooks everywhere, and they explain the reason behind the changing of the name that comes every century. Each girl that is renamed is named in honour of the first saint of the city. Perhaps because she was a woman, her true story is little known now. Perhaps because she was a woman, too, her story has been made more beautiful and more simple with time. The story that everyone knows now is an easy one. At the turn of the first century, the seas began to advance. The mud-banks that held back the oceans crumbled, and the waves ate away at the little town that was to become Galata. The town would have fallen into nothing. But a young girl, Sophia, had visions of what would happen. God told her how to resist the sea, and she obeyed. She prayed to God, the story runs, and because she was pure and a virgin He listened to her prayers. At the highest point of the highest tide, He listened. And so, because of the prayers of one

pure girl in a city of corruption, the seas began to recede.

It is a simple and innocent story, a tale of prayer and hope. But the manuscript that sits before Lucia now says something different. Other than the lines that everyone knows from the manuscript, the lines that were quoted across the ages, Lucia has known nothing. The traditional account ends the quote there. It continues by simply saying that Sophia gave herself to prayer; that she bound herself to God, and the city was saved. Her sacrifice is repeated every hundred years, the traditional story goes. Every century, for a year, a young virgin must marry herself to the ocean and to God. But the manuscript before her now says more. As Lucia reads, she sings to herself, trying to drown out the sound of her heart.

> *For many did dance beneath the waves, but one alone could match them. For she was Life and Death. And she spoke not, nor did she protest, nor did she accept the Devil's Pact. For Sophia alone was dumb. And she bowed against the ocean, even as it advanced. And although all prayed to the oceans and to God, only her silent dance could change the waves. Her Father was a Great Man, and her Mother wise. And they knew that words alone make Sin, for words alone make man. And so it was that on the night of Sophia's sacrifice they did cut out her tongue, and she alone was wise because she alone was dumb. And she danced with the Devil beneath the waves but said nothing, for she had learned to woo but not to Sin. And on the last day, the seas were high and they choked at the throat of the city. Those were times of great Contempt to God, and the city crumbled. But Sophia, who Could Not speak, was wise and good and the Priests of the city said Who Among Us Is Without Sin, and Who has shown only love. And the answer of her father and her mother both was, See she is Silent, see she knows only love. And so the priests said to the city, meet brine with blood.*

It is the sudden inrush of light from outside that pulls Lucia away from her reading. Peter is almost silent as he walks,

because he does not want to disturb her. But he cannot help the coming of the light. No one can.

"Sing on," he says as he advances on the girl. It is not a request. Still bent over the book, Lucia pretends to continue to read and as she pretends she sings. These are childhood songs of water and waves and light, songs she knows so well that she does not even notice what they mean. Quickly, Peter walks across the shaded space in the centre of the room and towards her. The manuscript is held in silver clamps, open at the page that she has reached, and even as he approaches she takes in a few more of the words of Thomas Burthen. She does not need to read them any more, though. Peter has the words engraved on his memory, and when he sees what she is reading he begins to quote them without even trying to read the frantic scrawl of the priest from long ago.

"And so they cut her at the throat, and they cut her at the wrists, and the tide of her blood met the tide of the waves. And she exhausted the ocean with her dance. And at last the seas gave way, because life is sin but silent life is faith... Beautiful words, Lucia. A little out-of-hours reading for you. I'm so glad to find you here. I always wanted you to understand, but I didn't know how to tell you. It takes death to make life. How clever of you to find out for yourself. "

Slowly, he reaches his arms around both sides of the girl, and closes the book in front of her gently. Then, with one hand, he pulls back her hair so tightly that it hurts a little.

"You've found out my little secret," he says. "I'm glad. It's always good to share. I've wanted to show you this room for a long time. But... well, I must admit I'm a little sad you've gone *this* far. Reading about the festivities. Reading about the truth. You've looked where you shouldn't have."

He shrugs.

"It's sad. I was going to make love to you, Lucia. It would have been so beautiful, and I know it's what you wanted. When I saw you were in here, I hoped I would not be too late. You've read the truth, though, now. I shouldn't want to make love to anyone who's read the truth. You're not

pure any more, not like you were. But you are still beautiful, and it would be a shame for you to die."

Peter pulls once more at Lucia's hair, dragging it backwards. Her arms are free, but she does not move them. There is nothing for her to do except close her eyes.

"Do you read the papers, my dear? Have you read about God's work? All these nice girls, learning how to drown. It's like the past, isn't it? But the seas are still rising, aren't they… The buildings are still falling. I've told you it would be a shame to lose you now, pure or not. You know so much. I'd like to show you more, if you don't mind. I'd like to take you to church. You know enough now, you might as well know everything."

He smiles, behind Lucia's back.

"You can say no if you want to. Of course you can. I'm a kind man. A quick death, or – the chance to share. In some ways, I'm uncomfortable with both. I wish we could have just made love, and ended it there. I wish you hadn't read the truth. But you've gone too far, and now you have to make a choice. I'll show you things not many people know. I'll share things with you that you might not *want* to know. But sometimes you have no choice. Death, or discovery. You might not want either. But sometimes, whatever we choose, we regret."

At this, Lucia opens her eyes and looks straight ahead of her. She can feel the warmth of the man behind her, his surprising strength. There is nothing for her to do now. Desperately, she tries to smile.

"I'd like to see it," she says. "I'd like to see everything."

She turns to face him. He does not tie her hands, but he holds her firmly by one wrist as he leads her from the inner library and out into the world. Outside, it is raining a little. Because he is kind, he gives her his coat on the condition that she does not try to run.

The rain has turned to sleet by the time they reach the old church. The night was warmer than the day that is now

coming; unusually, the sunrise brings about a sudden chill, as a cold wind blows up from the north. All the while that they have been walking, Peter has asked Lucia to continue singing. It makes him feel calm, he says. Perhaps it pleases him, too, because it means that none of the few strangers who pass them in the street question what he is doing. Perhaps they would see her fear if they looked in her eyes, but most people think that no one who sings is truly afraid.

It delighted Peter when he first heard her singing, and it delights him now. She is a good girl, and the songs that she knows from childhood are beautiful and familiar to him. He is pleased, in particular, to find that she knows the songs of the seasons that are sung in every church. She must have been a beautiful little girl, with a wonderful little voice. As he leads the way, forcing her forwards, he asks her to sing the simple songs that the choirs sing at the quarters of the year. Spring, Summer, Autumn, Winter... It is good to be guided by something familiar, it is good to know the music as he walks.

Lucia sings her childish song softly, and when her voice fades Peter pulls at her hair and asks her to wake up. There are great things to see and he is eager to show her them. When they reach the abandoned streets that have been eaten by the sea, however, Lucia's voice falters and dies. She has not been in this area for years. Very few people come here. Even the homeless are wary of living in the houses on these streets: afraid of the high tides and the crumbling foundations. Squalid, rotten sandbags line most doorways, green with mould and swollen with water. Very soon, she is entirely lost in her own city, walking down streets that mean nothing to her, looking at flaked-away advertisements for ancient medicines that have half-collapsed, plasterwork that is cracked with dark veins.

Even from this distance, deep in the broken centre of the city, Lucia and Peter can hear the drums start up with the dawn. This is a rhythm that will last throughout the day. Every radio in the city will be tuned to the rhythm. Drummers will beat it out, children will walk to its rhythms, lovers will love to it. This is the heartbeat of the

city. A hundred years ago, two hundred years ago, it was played out by bands that marched around the streets. Today, it dominates everything still more. If Lucia or Peter could hear any radio station, they would realise more fully the strangeness of it. The stations are not silent; they play their music, read their news. But underneath everything is the heartbeat, a drum-weight that the pair hear in the distance as they make their way to the church. It started with the first birdsong, and it swills around the city, ceaselessly.

When they enter the church Peter locks the doors and then lets Lucia go free. He is glad to let her go, surprised because he feels a little out of breath. He pretends to himself that this is excitement, but really it is exhaustion.

"We've hours to kill," he says. "Let me tell you a little about history."

"Go on."

Lucia looks around at the water-marred walls, then up at the perfect stained glass. With the calm certainty of someone who has created his own space, Peter pulls out a book from the piles that are scattered here and there across the church. Sitting Lucia down, he opens up the book. It is wide and heavy, and stretches across both of their laps, and he remembers the tender times when he was young and the person he called mother would read to him.

"Do you like stories?" he asks. "I wrote this myself. Drew the pictures, and the words. It was important to get it all down. Not many people have the gift."

Inside the leather binding of the book, the pages are dry with the sad dryness of paper that has become clotted a little with damp. The ink is slightly smeared, but still readable. The librarian writes in a clean, perfect script. Its perfect nature is only enhanced by the fact that the water has touched it. On the left hand pages, he has written the words that he discovered so long ago; words he has heard in his mind for years. The right hand pages are saved for illustrations. These are clumsy sketches, and even in her terror Lucia finds it hard to believe that the same person could have written so perfectly and drawn so gracelessly.

There are drawings of devils and angels, of kneeling apes and risen gods. Although they are poorly drawn there is something disturbing about all of them, and she is reminded of the pictures of primitive people.

"I confess I'm not much of an artist."

Peter is smiling as he says this, with the confidence that he is being modest.

"I didn't try to capture the world as it is," he says. "These drawings are meant to be souls. Look, you see. As I say, I'm not much of an artist. But I see so much, Lucia. These are the only angels you'll ever see. I know what they look like. If you're patient, perhaps, we'll read all through the book. If you're patient, I'll show you God."

Lucia does not speak unless Peter tells her to. When he gives her the order, she speaks because she has no choice. Otherwise the slaps would become punches, the pain would become torture. And although he has little interest in what the girl has to say, Peter *is* eager for her to speak. He wants her to read out his words.

"I wrote this for a woman to speak," he says. "It's a tradition. She's not here yet, but it's good to practice. But don't get above yourself, will you. You're very lucky. I've given you the chance to read these words. But don't dare think they're for you. They are only really for one girl. Try and sound innocent as you read, won't you? I know it will be difficult, but try."

As Lucia reads from the book, her voice wavering and soft, Peter tries to imagine that the words are being read by someone else.

The pages that Lucia reads are an outline of the truth that Peter knows. As he hears them read, he tries hard to catch the glints of light that he knows are in his words. They are written in the spaces between the words, he thinks. The words themselves just muddy the water. But without them, there would be no water and there would be no way of holding back the waves.

The book, Lucia soon realises, is little more than a collection of familiar phrases from books she knows well and childhood songs that are familiar to her. They seem to

have nothing in common apart from the fact that they are all preoccupied with the waves. There are quotes from monks in the middle ages, tied close to quotes from scientists about the nature of the sea. There are brief sermons about the moon, coupled with observations about the nature of man. In the distance, the drums can still be heard and Peter taps out their rhythm against the vein on her neck.

"The oceans are necessarily tied to the moon and the moon has an Unnatural Force upon them: Hence, the moon – being above nature – may be regarded as a kind of God. If the moon is God – as the ancients agree – then sacrifices must be made."

Then, a space in the text marked with a star.

"And so said Saint Matthius, To Hold Back The Waves Is The Greatest Gift."

On the opposing page, swirls of waves rising up and down, like a child's drawing, with a crescent moon above.

As the pages are turned, Lucia begins to understand the message in the book. The different quotes are tied together clumsily, but because of that their knotting has more force, every phrase adding more tension and weight to the whole. The pictures, too, become stronger with every page turned. They are still ugly and clumsily drawn, but she begins to see a connection between them. The crouched down apes or the wing-spread angels all stand beneath the drawing of a moon. And on every page, the moon is given more solidity. At the beginning, it is the slightest crescent. But with every page that is turned, by the librarian sitting beside her, the moon becomes more full.

The two sit there for over an hour, reading through the book. The pages feel like rough skin between her fingers, but although they are thick there are perhaps a hundred, most covered with these stitched together phrases. Every now and then, as she reads, the librarian catches her at the wrist briefly. He wants her to read, he tells her, but he doesn't want her to be too passionate about it. He doesn't want her to take all the strength away from the words, and her sin is so great that if she reads too passionately she

might sully the book. And remember, he says, the words are for another. They are not for you.

"Let me tell you first of the still oceans, and of the dead. They say there are seas in Africa that do not rise or fall. They say these seas are as dead and as thick as blood. These Dead Seas have no waves, and the natives who live in these lands say that life came from the oceans, and that this is what made them still. They say that the oceans were once inhabited by demons. But the demons are dead, and their death killed the sea." Peter turns the page. Here they reach the last of the writing. On this page alone, Peter has written his own thoughts. "Dead seas? Dead moon. Dead waves. Dead soul? Meet brine with blood."

The rest of the page is blank.

Lucia is surprised and relieved when she comes to this abrupt end in the writing, some pages before the end of the book. The quotes still weigh heavy in her head and bubble in her blood, cramping her muscles. Her hands are shaking slightly.

"You did a good job," says Peter. "I bet you were a good girl at school."

"I'm sorry?"

"That's not good enough. Sorry isn't good enough. If only you'd stayed pure. You've probably guessed it all, haven't you? It's so funny. I didn't even have to write a thing myself. I just read what others wrote, and here we have it. The soul of the city. The answer to our prayers. It's very interesting, isn't it? Turn the page."

On the next page there is no handwriting at all. Instead, Peter has turned the remaining pages of the book into a kind of scrapbook. Here, the accounts of the murders one hundred years ago are recorded, in the clipped neat tones of ancient newspapers. The articles are glued in clumsily, but the messages they state are plain. Seven murders in seven days.

"Others have had the same idea, you see," Peter says. "The greatest artists, the greatest prophets, are always inspired by the clumsy past. Others understood it once. I don't know who. No one knows who. But others figured

out most of it. In order to hold back the waves, you have to kill. Of course you do. That's why they're rising so much, you see. Because they want life. There is something beneath the sea. *He* is angry, *He* is lonely. But the sad thing is, *these* lives were in vain. The sacrifices that were made a hundred years ago, at least. Completely in vain. They held back the waves a little, I suppose, but they were pointless in the end. I think they made it worse, if anything."

Outside, the sleet has turned to snow now and the stained glass is becoming clouded with white, which darkens the different colours of the panes and shadows the room with imperfect shadows where the snow has clustered or fallen away.

"You see, whoever he was – let's assume he was a man, no woman could be strong like that – he realised that we needed to make sacrifices. But he didn't understand what the ancients understood. Perhaps three hundred years ago, they did it right. There aren't enough records to tell me that. But the century that followed, there was nothing. And then the seas began to rise, of course they did. And even though, a hundred years ago, someone had the right idea, it all went wrong at the last. That's why the last century has been so painful to everyone. To you, to me. He killed, and killed again. Bravo. But he failed at the end."

Peter smiles, his lips dry and cracked in the cold of the old abandoned church.

"They say it's a small world. Well, I don't know about that. But it's a small city, isn't it? It's amazing how few people there are. Sometimes, in the library, it seems I know everyone. The rat-like men who look for filth, the pure-bred girls who seek romance, the dry-boned scientists who tie their minds in knots. I knew she would come, and she did. The rock on which it's all built. Rebecca. She'll be here later. Not much of a girl in herself, in truth. A trifle – mindless. Probably a good thing. But she has friends in the highest places. She told me so herself. She's bringing a friend today. She's going to introduce me. Perhaps you've met her already."

Pausing, he takes one of Lucia's hands, looking at her close-bitten fingernails.

"Sophia. Such a lovely name. The only pure girl. *They did cut out her tongue, and she alone was wise.* Wisdom. It's the greatest gift of all, I've always thought." He smiles. "You're in on it now, aren't you? We need her. She will understand. I'll make her understand. It's what I was born for, if I was born at all."

At this, Peter smiles to himself. Sometimes it feels as though he never stopped being born. The pain that comes in waves, and then abates. He sits there for a moment, and then he asks the girl to sing again. Outside, in the far distance, the drums are continuing and he makes her sing familiar songs to the rhythms far away. The words don't quite fit the heartbeat-rhythm, but he knows she'll make them fit, even if she has to break the spines of phrases to make them know their place.

Chapter Seven.

Celice knew everyone, but pretended to know no-one. That is the job of a photographer, and she was training to be one. She was taught it from the start. Remain obscure, remain part of the background. Simply take the images. And so, she had not been surprised when she was asked by Erin to take a series of photographs for a friend. From the first, when she met Rebecca, there had been a connection: the kind that comes with two people who have led lives of similar blankness. The commission had been connected to blankness, as well. Seven photographs of women, with their faces smeared away. A simple process, scratching holes in negatives. The woman could be anyone, Rebecca explained. That was the point. The picture had to represent everyone.

Often it is dangerous to say too much, but sometimes it is dangerous too to be quiet. As Peter now leafs through the photographs that remain in his possession, he feels a sense of sorrow and of wonder at how neatly everything has progressed. There are only three photographs left, now. The other four were burned away, one after another with each death. It was only appropriate that the woman who took the photographs should be the first to die. She chose her own face for the pictures, and so she too had to be scratched out. It had been so gratifying to watch the girl fall under. She had taken the drugs gladly, calling them part of her payment. At the last, nobody could have called her anything but happy. He had put her in touch with her spiritual side, he had put her in contact with God.

As Peter is sitting with Lucia, Rebecca is making her way towards the church with an old schoolfriend she has scarcely talked to for years. Sophia was always a quiet girl, easy to manipulate. Unusually beautiful, she had been disliked for that from an early age. There wasn't much else of her to dislike. She was an empty girl, Rebecca thinks. She

still is. A nothing, a receptacle. Or – how was it that Peter put it? – a lens. It is necessary for a person to be completely empty to be a lens like that. Otherwise, how can the light of God be truly focused through them? Now, the quiet girl is following Rebecca gladly. She is not used to being treated like royalty, and the novelty has yet to wear off. While this week has seen her almost worshipped by the great and the good among the city, that hasn't really meant much to her. It means so much more to be treated with deference by someone she has known since she was a child; known, and subtly hated with the hatred of someone who is envious of what she cannot have.

Sophia has not told anyone where she is going. She has no duty to do so, no obligation until Saturday, when she must rise again on the high stand in the central square and give her final prayer. The only obligation that she has at this moment is to keep the crown wound around her dark and sodden hair, and swear to anyone who asks that she has given herself to God alone. Here, as she walks, there are very few people to see and nobody even seems to notice the crown. She walks through water-numbed streets, smiling at Rebecca, who is inventing happy memories of a shared past together. Both of them know that this past is a lie. The only things they ever shared as children were teachers. They were never really friends.

"It must be exciting to be Queen of the City."

This comes from nowhere, in the middle of a conversation about the past.

"I don't know what it means, really."

"But just think." Rebecca breathes against the rain. "It means everything. All of this… It's all yours, isn't it? You own everything."

In a sense that's true. But in another sense, Sophia knows, she owns nothing at all. Nothing is in her name. The silver and the silence and the worship, all of those are just for Galata itself. She is only a bride, owned by the place where she was born, married to the streets and the stone. She tries to say as much, but it comes out wrong and Rebecca almost loses her friendliness at the answer. She cannot bear to hear

the stupidity of the girl, her false modesty that is really nothing more than arrogance. Soon, as they walk in the streets towards the river, they find themselves wading up to their ankles in water. The water is high now, only two days away from the full moon, with the tide lulling and pressing against the cobbles.

By the time that the pair reach the church, on a street where the water is almost ankle-deep, the sun has risen completely. It was a midwinter dawn, very slow and very grey as though the world barely had enough strength within it to keep turning. Here, there are pictures everywhere but even the graffiti is old. The artists, disappointed at how quickly the water claims their paintings, have given up and moved their attention to other streets where the water has yet to properly break through. What pictures there are, Sophia cannot help but notice, are of dark-haired women. They are paintings of the river's bride, made close to the water. Partly perhaps they are sad attempts to hold back the tide by offering it a wife. If Sophia can help by coming this close to the water, she thinks, she is happy to do so. Rebecca has told her that she can. She has suggested that it is only by getting close to the water that the girl can hope to give it the respect it deserves. People don't realise, she has kept on saying. People don't understand. She wants her old friend to understand.

When they reach the church the pair have to kick aside some sandbags that the librarian has stood up against the closed door to keep away the river until the time is right. As they do so, and open the door, the water comes pouring in with them until in very little time the entire inside of the church is ankle-deep in scum-covered brine. Peter sees this happen but he does not mind because he knows that it is time. He welcomes Sophia in with an eager sort of deference and for the first time Rebecca finds herself disliking the man who has taught her so much about God. Soon that dislike falls away. Because while Peter takes Sophia's hand with a tender worship, he does not let go. Instead, he holds her firmly.

"So you think you know about tides," he says in a voice

that is sweet and surprisingly quiet. "Let me tell you a thing or two about tides…"

Carefully, holding the girl by the wrists, he sits her down at the front of the church facing towards the circle of light that shines colours and grey down calmly upon them all. Beside her, Lucia is sitting with her arms tied, looking at everything but saying nothing because her mouth is taped shut.

Far from the church, the feast has begun. The streets are littered with people and the only order, even now, is found in the straight lines of the tables that line every road of the old town that has not been wrecked by water. It is perhaps ten in the morning when Joseph leaves his home and makes his way towards these feasting tables, which are half full already and crowded with food. Everywhere the old, men and women who are either alone or too decrepit for sex, are preparing the meal. It is beautiful to see it happening. Every house, every flat above every shop has prepared something. Part of the wonder of the feast is its ramshackle nature. This is not just some grand meal of hot flesh, an over-extravagant lunch for the city. Instead, people have simply offered what they have, cooked or uncooked, prepared or unprepared. The tables are covered with chocolate and meat and crisps and vegetables, cut apples or old tangerines, imported fruit from foreign countries. At the ends of every street, and in the middle of most, are barbecues; strong fires, across which are strung taut wires pierced with kebabs, the meat on the outside burnt but on the inside cool. Bottles of wine stand on every table, cheap or expensive, old or new. Joseph stands alone and cold beside a leering old woman and trades some flirtation for food.

As he eats, warily consuming cold food and crisps and staying away from the stomach-cramping meat that is burning on every fire, Joseph walks up and down the streets and looks out at the world. There is no shelter from the rain, except for the occasional umbrella that is held up by

one hand here and there along the street. Most people are happy to take in the water, to allow themselves to get wet and let their food get soaked. That is nature's way, and the way it should be today. Although Joseph is exhausted, he is smiling now, happy to see so many people celebrating what it is to be alive. In part, he is happy just because it almost makes him feel as though he is himself alive. For too many years now, he has felt dead inside, as cold in his heart as this frozen meat stays while it burns in suspension above the fires.

Joseph cannot forget the case, of course. His mind is filled with thoughts of silver, swollen bodies, swollen paper. But there is nothing for him to do at this moment. He spent the night exploring the churches, looking at faces and thinking about the present and the past. He has done all that he can, at least until J. D. wakes up. Nonetheless, he is still wide awake and wholly empty. He should feel more about the murders, he knows that. But in truth he has never felt the same about death, not since the death of Alicia. She had been in the wrong place at the wrong time.

It is amazing how much a silencer can numb the sound of gunshots. The man had entered their apartment without a sound, and Joseph's wife had died voiceless while he had shaved in the next room. Even lying in hospital, his arm pinned up and numbed to sleep, Joseph had had to struggle to remember the case that had led to his wife's murder. A drugs bust. They said that the murderer's wife had died, shot by the police as she scurried away, high on tinfoil fantasies. Joseph, a man who sees little order in anything, can at least appreciate the symmetry in his own wife's death. The murderer had been sentenced to life. Apparently in prison he had taken up with God, bowing his head every Sunday, singing his heart out with the rest of them. It must be nice to have that, Joseph thinks.

The children join the old in taking part in the first of the feast. Their parents are still in bed. Today is a day when they are supposed to let their children run free. Let them murder each other if they want to, while their parents huddle upstairs. In fact, murder is the last thing on any

child's mind today. They are feasting on forbidden food, guzzling down sugar and blending it with alcohol. Most are far too young to appreciate the taste, but they are keen to experience the effects. As Joseph walks, he sees a group of children who cannot be more than eight or nine. There are perhaps ten of them, standing together. They have found metal bowls from somewhere, mess-bowls that make him think of war, even though he has never experienced war. In every one of these bowls is some sort of sweet cereal, but in place of milk each bowl is filled to the brim with dark red wine. The cereal catches in their teeth, and when they smile it looks as though their gums are dripping blood.

The fifth day is the day of man. In most of the city this means it is a day of music; a morning of singing, and of brass bands playing while people devour food. It is a day to forget about inhibitions completely; to unpin your nervousness, to release yourself. It is also a time to mark yourself and make sure you are remembered. One truth about being alive is that you will be quickly forgotten, and the nametags and dark marks that many are scrawling on the tall walls and elegant curlicues of ancient stone are a testament to this. They are daubs and sketches and brief reflections, swirls of graffiti that are meant only to note that the person who has marked them was alive, is alive at this moment. Market stalls are making insane amounts of money selling marker pens. Children are chalking their own features over old statues, making circlets of blue or green chalk in blank eyes. The feast goes on, but while they are eating many take brief breaks to etch on the walls. By noon most people are full up to their throats, anyway. The food will be out on the tables all day. Old chairs will line the streets. But most of the feasting is done.

The marks that people make are not anything that could be predicted. A hundred years ago, two hundred years ago, it was in many ways the same. Different figures left their symbols on the stone. But back then, a century in the past,

the symbols were all of chalk and the hallmarks of life collapsed in the next strong rainfall. Now, aware that the city does not need respect, the people are treating it like a dying animal that cannot fight back. The nasty dark tags of the young are being smeared over shop windows. Declarations of love, but also of hatred are noted everywhere. Joseph, who has eaten now, walks the city and as he walks he grows to realise that the drawings are different in the different streets. In Thamin road there are daubs of animals, living or dying. In Gowyim Alley, deep in the foreign part of the city, are strange alien etchings. Someone here has written over and over 'man is now here', or 'man is nowhere'. The writing is odd, with the letters marked above and below with accents that have no place in the words. In one place he sees a map drawn that looks familiar but that he cannot understand, until he realises that the unnamed streets are a near-precise mirroring of the streets of his city.

When it has turned one in the afternoon, Joseph finally breaks and decides that he will call on J. D. He feels uncomfortable doing so; walking up the clean, sane path, knocking on a door that is as yet unmarked by the swathes of swirls that are cutting through the city. The children are out, running the streets presumably, but the photographs that he sees when he walks into the living room make him uncomfortable. He cannot forget Alicia's swollen belly. Here, surrounded by the photographs, he finds himself staring at Cassandra's figure as she walks across the room. The curve of her hips and the calm of her walk as she steps over toys and invites him to sit. She does not know how to talk to him and it is clear that she does not want to talk to him; that she resents him somehow for being part of the search which is obsessing her lover, today of all days. For a moment, Joseph feels responsible somehow for the murders, as though even by visiting the home he is bringing the threat of death near. He sees Cass talking, but he hardly hears the words. He imagines her dead, and his own life alive. For a moment, he tries to twist the world, to make this woman into his own lost lover. Sensing this, perhaps,

Cass leaves the room as soon as J. D. arrives. She has things to do, she says nervously. Perhaps she is planning on going outside, leaving her mark on the day. She looks tired enough but alert enough to do anything.

When he comes out, J. D. is unshaven and his teeth are dirty with the scum of too much drink and not enough sleep. As though he is proud of this, he keeps on smiling, a little manic through the force of the day. After they have sat in the room for barely any time, the two of them go outside and into the street. Joseph notes to himself that J. D. does not even bother to say goodbye to his wife. She is angry with him for leaving her. That much is plain and ugly to see. She is angry that she must stay alone, while her other friends are hunched with their lovers. She does not trust Joseph, something he understands because he does not trust himself. Although Cass knows that they are working together, part of her mind can't help wondering. Why would a married man want to be apart from his wife, on this day? As they walk down the street, she is watching them walk from between the thin curtains that frame her bedroom window, thinking of what they could be up to, the places that they might be going together. Eventually they find a place to sit and J. D. asks him what his plans might be, if he has any at all.

"I want to go back."

The two of them are drinking coffee now on Gowyim street, dark foreign coffee that tastes as though it must have been brewed in another, warmer country. It burns their throats and it invigorates their thoughts, shaking them into a wakefulness that catches them by surprise, their minds knotting and aching with sudden awareness.

"I want to go back to Celice's. I want to check again."

J. D. does not know much, but he can tell that Joseph has some kind of idea. He nods his head and they stand, wired still on the caffeine thrill. Slowly, looking at every face as though they might be given some clue just through catching a glance of a stranger's eye, they walk through the roads to the main body of the river. The barges into the centre of the city are crowded with people, mostly couples.

This late in the day, the owners of the boats have given up trying to prevent people from attempting to make their marks. Joseph is saddened by the ugliness of the graffiti everywhere. He had hoped that people would be capable of more; of beautiful pictures, eloquent words. But all that shows, everywhere, are scrawls and tags in black marker-pen, mis-spelt declarations of love, badly drawn smiling faces that are little more than circles and dots.

You can tell a true citizen of Galata by the way he looks. It is not in the features, because they have become smeared by ages. Different races have come and gone, and the fair skin, thin bones and dark hair that characterised the people for centuries have blurred into the colouring and curves of other races. But there are in the faces of the true citizens here certain qualities that tourists do not have. A guilelessness that is wholly deceptive, a faint expression of calm that Joseph sometimes thinks could just be read as emptiness. It is more noticeable as they reach the centre, where the true Galatans merge with the occasional, frightened tourist. The people from the city, beyond the age of childhood, tend to wear a certain expression that reminds of nothing more than a beautiful woman aware that her beauty is fading fast. There is that desperation, that sadness coupled with arrogance. Joseph loves to see it as he walks away from the barge, along the narrow street that leads to the apartment where the party began for him.

Paul is not alone when the two men arrive. His money buys him drink, and the drink has brought him company; a woman who is overly made up, her lips smeared thick with lipstick that is bright and seems as permanent as paint. It is the woman who answers the door, and the two men are immediately put on their guard by her. She is dressed like a caricature, her skirt too short and her blouse half unbuttoned. The smile seems stuck on her face, and they quickly realise that is because it is. Her lips are not smiling, but her painted expression suggests that they are. She

introduces herself as Karma, pronouncing it to sound like Calmer. Perhaps she has been paid for. Whatever the truth is, Paul seems neither glad not irritated to see them. He tells the falsely smiling woman to go to his room and she walks off slowly, her hands slightly open as though she were trying to hold the air.

Soon the three are settled in the living room. Outside the house, people are walking up and down the streets, many of them playing music of some form or other. From the radios, the incessant beat goes on. Above it, there are harmonicas, but there are also loudspeakers that declare melodies. Somewhere in a distance a man is shrieking out his thoughts on God. His words are ridiculously high-pitched, and Paul thinks how absurd religion sounds when it is preached in such a desperate falsetto. Fairly rapidly he slams closed the shutters so that the room is almost entirely dark, and switches on the two lamps that sit on two small tables on either side of the table where the three sit. In this numb twilight he lights a cigarette and offers one to each of the two men, who take them. Joseph doesn't smoke, not really, but he likes to see the smoke play when it is half-dark like this and so he breathes it in and holds it and then lets it swirl out again, nudging it towards the light with the pressure from his lips. It is perhaps the smoke and the twilight that make him notice for the first time more formally the many photographs that are on the walls.

"You like them?" Paul asks. "The only good thing Celice ever did, if you ask me." He smiles. The photographs are frequently of women, many of them naked in a way that is almost art but not quite. "She took a lot of 'art' photographs." He pronounces the word with a curled sort of sneer that is almost laughter, though not of a pleasant kind.

"They're beautiful," says Joseph, not meaning it. There is something awkward and submissive about the photographs, as though the women in them are not entirely comfortable with what they are being asked to do.

"She's got drawers full of them," says Paul. "Her legacy."

Standing up, he walks into Celice's room and comes back

with five books of photographs. The three men leaf through these books, the black and white photographs held in by plastic that shines in the low light. Beside each of the photographs is a date, neatly written in dark pencil with expensively taught handwriting. As they read, the three men cannot help noticing one thing that Paul is the first to observe.

"She had a dirty little mind."

The photographs start relatively innocently. There are naked women, naked men, pictures taken in art classes. But soon they become preoccupied with one thing. The pictures of men fall away into nothing, and then there are only pictures of women. Young, old, sometimes too young to be photographed in the way that they have been. At first, their expressions are shown to the full, sometimes in close up. Even in these photographs, there is an uncomfortable blankness, an emptiness in their eyes. All of them are taken in an empty room, a very large room. If it is a class, J. D. thinks, then it is a class with only one pupil. In the third book, though, that all changes. Because from the beginning, the faces are not merely blank because the models are showing no expression. They are blank because the faces themselves have been smeared away, as though the negatives have been scratched into nothingness.

A little way into the third volume, the pictures change again. Now, the photographs have been taken outside, in the countryside. Joseph recognises the place where the images are set. It is a little down from the city, an area where not many people go. Immediately before the ocean begins, the river smears into the sea in a space where there are no houses, a grubby sad marshland haunted only by small trees and weeds. All of the photographs are taken at night by flash photography, which shows the whole world as darkness except for the immediate close dazzle of a naked body near to the waters and faceless. Quickly, Joseph understands that all of the photographs in this third book are of the same girl. Her face too is blurred into nothing, but he gets the feeling she is smiling. There is nothing unhappy about these pictures, regardless of the poses; poses

where she is bowing, kneeling at the water's edge. When he can turn away from the pictures, he sees that Paul has turned away.

"A man has some standards," he says, and from this Joseph realises for the first time that this is Celice, thinner than he thought she would be. They say that photographs add weight to a person, but perhaps the quick flash of light against darkness has stripped weight away from the girl. Her curves are all shadows and sharp lines.

The pictures in this third book do not seem to lead anywhere. There is no order to them, and there are no dates beside any of them. All that they have in common is that they are of the same girl, and they are at night. The stars are not shown by the flash, but the moon sometimes reveals itself, here and there in different phases.

The last half of the book is taken up with negatives, stretched beneath the plastic sheets in strips. At times there are pictures that have somehow been developed in negative, Joseph doesn't know how. In these pictures, the night sky is almost white, the body's curves inverse in their patterns of light and dark. Always, they are of the same figure, pictures of a girl who is now dead. Pictures singing with life. The pictures themselves are not well taken. Whoever took them didn't have an artist's eye; no matter how well the girl posed, there is a certain clumsiness about them. But when the men move on to the next and final volume, all that changes for one final time. Because here, the pictures are very beautiful, impeccably shot. They are, it becomes immediately apparent, all photographs of churches. The pictures are not just one church; many different buildings, taken inside and out; windows and high gothic towers, or at times the blunt clumsiness of modern buildings from the outskirts. There are no strips of negatives here. But all of the photographs, without exception, are black and white, and all have been developed in negative. The final photograph here is the only one which shows a figure. The naked girl, standing in the dark/light of a stained glass window. In her hair, they can just make out the dark circlet of a silver crown.

There is no apparent reason why these photographs should have been developed like this. It must clearly have taken a lot of effort, Joseph thinks, to invert the negatives in such a way; to turn light to dark, and dark to light. To create something that is at once a church, and at the same time…

"I don't know why she did this," says Paul. "She never was religious. None of us were. But she developed this fondness, recently. I teased her for it, said that she'd got God. Said she'd seen the light. But she always said that wasn't it. She told me she was looking for the opposite of light. That's what the negatives are all about, I suppose."

The opposite of churches.

Chapter Eight.

The oldest texts say it as well as Peter ever could. There was a wonderful point in the history of Galata, and that was the time which made the city great. Three hundred years in which the city soared and grew, thriving by the waters. Artists went to the city, working for the sake of God. But while the best of art is declared in the name of God, it was never quite that simple. Those great years, early in the life of the city, everything seemed to work together. The tides were strong, but that strength took nothing away from the place. The cancer that has come in now, carried on saltwater and eating away at stone, was not heard of then. Instead, the seas brought nothing but gifts. From the depths, they offered up life; food that kept the city in life. As importantly, the sea carried in ships from far away. The gold and faith of warmer lands, Moorish curls that kissed the stone and dignified arches that marked the thin streets. The sea seemed to serve them in every way. The city was gripped by a kind sort of mania, which made everywhere alive, vivid with ideas. But there comes a point, always, where elation turns to madness.

There is something about faith, Peter thinks, that very few people seem to recognise. In order to truly understand, you have to look backwards, always backwards. True faith means knowing how much to give, and what to offer up. He has seen the way this week has progressed for most people. Mass hysteria, wave after breaking wave. The people are destroying the city around them. It has hurt him to see it happening. Even now, deep in the church, he knows what the people outside are doing. Scratching their marks over ancient paintings. Daubing meaningless palimpsests across the ancient arches. They don't know what their actions truly mean. It is as though they are fighting against the sea, trying to destroy the buildings before the waves can win. None of them seem to realise the truth of it. Even if he could explain to them, they wouldn't listen. These people, who think nothing of destroying the beauty around them. They would be angry at him, angry at his love.

"Look at her. Just what we needed. Emptiness at last."

The young girl at the front of the church has her head up. She is murmuring, although she has made sure that you cannot hear the words. Carelessly, Peter walks to one of the piles of books and picks up an ancient volume. He opens it, looking up first at the group around him. They are all there now, the people who have the courage to share. Daniel and John sit a little behind the women. Rebecca holds on to Sophia, with one stern hand. Lucia is fluttering her eyes a little, as though she is looking for a way out. She doesn't realise that Peter *is* the way.

The words are written in an ugly kind of Latin, peppered here and there with old phrases from his own language. The book is handwritten and it has been kept locked away for more than four hundred years. The old man in charge of the library had said it was for the best. He had not understood the truth. If you have control of the words, Peter knows, then you have control of the world.

"Rebecca, sweetness. Lucia. Every one of you. Daniel, John. Even Sophia. I know what you are thinking. It's so far from the truth, it's hard for me to answer it. But I know what you're thinking, and I'll try my best. My friends, you think I'm killing these people. No, don't deny it. Even you, Rebecca. Even pretty little Lucia, my best and my kindest friend. You think I'm a murderer. But listen to this. These, believe me, are the nearest words you'll ever get to God. The writing's clumsy. The writer wasn't what we'd call — educated. But what he wrote... This is the last prayer of Saint Sophia. Tangled up of course. I don't say it's word for word. But hers was not a sacrifice, understand that. It was a privilege. Absolutely."

Smiling, he takes the book over to the front of the church, sitting down with his back against the high stone of the altar.

"It's funny. There was a saying my 'mother' used to share with me sometimes. Caught beneath the devil and the deep

blue sea. She didn't understand how close she was to the truth. The sea has been growing mad, hasn't it? The oceans have been growing mad. And I'll tell you why. We're making it easy for Him."

Peter smiles.

"We're giving it all up to the Devil. He was put there to serve us, deep beneath the sea. God told him to make the tides for us, to make this city great. But he always wanted more. God knew that, I know that. We shouldn't be breaking the city apart for him. We should be working against Him, making Him work for us. That's how it was always meant to be, that's how the waves should work. He's trying to madden us all with the dance of the waves. And Heaven knows, it looks like he's succeeding. But let's not forget, it was God at first who put the devil there beneath the waves…"

He strokes the book as though he is stroking a child's hair, and then he begins to read, translating the words as he reads. Throughout, he reads slowly and awkwardly, leaving little breaks while he pauses to work out the words. That's quite alright, he thinks. Even the waves need to take a break, within each turning of the tides.

"Such pretty words. Nine hundred years old, this story. 'And when she was gone beneath the waves, there was a day of madness and fury, a day of the devil and a day of the damned. The seas rose high and took her body and soul, and she danced with the devil beneath the waves. But *she* danced with the strength of Christ stern within her. For with every other sacrifice, the *four* that went before, the devil who serves but who wants to rule had gained strength. With every day of offering, the oceans had grown stronger, the tides had gained weight. The dead had danced with the devil, but the demon in the sea had not been weakened. For these sacrifices had been right in spirit but *wrong in judgement*. And still with every sacrifice the dark grew more great and the tides more furious. But at the last, after the death of the babe-in-arms, the true and the wise of the city understood. Even the innocent, if they could answer the seduction of the waves, would be corrupted. The sacrifices

had been made to tire the devil of the ocean's deep, He who had served but sought to Rule. But the devil had tempted the bodies he took with *sweet words and sustenance*, had asked the dead to give up God and give themselves to the seething tides. And the dead had answered yes, for are we not all *mortal and weak*?

"But Sophia alone did not cease in her dance beneath the sea. She danced with the devil until he tired, exhausted by her strength and by the strength of God within her. The devil wooed her with the song of the sea, but she did not answer him. For they had cut out her tongue and *she alone* was dumb, and would not answer yes to dark, and would not rest when the devil demanded rest. And so the devil lost the dance, and with that the waves gave up their fury. And on the day that followed the sea was calm and the men and women of the city went to the ocean's edge, where the fury had been so great the day before that it had *broken the stones of the harbour*. They stood and gave praise, for their city was saved. And as they sang praise, the stillness of the oceans began to stir. One by one, the five rose from the deep. Tears flowed from the eyes of those who had given themselves to the devil, but these were tears of joy. And the last to rise was Saint Sophia, singing as she rose. For in her mouth was a tongue of light, which sang the purest songs."

Smiling, Peter moves forward to stroke Sophia's hair as he reads.

"A tongue of light. But listen. After she sang, she spoke. She said a few words. 'I have danced the devil into nothing, danced him until he fell. His force is gone, the fury of the waves exhausted. The devil will serve you again, and the oceans be your slave, and be the slave of God.'"

Peter closes the book, throwing the ancient text onto a swollen wooden bench.

"And all because of a night of dancing. Dancing the devil down into submission. It's not a privilege offered to many, is it? It will mean that you have to be brave. Please tell me you are brave, Sophia. They say he's an excellent partner."

It is after dark when the two men leave the apartment. With them, they carry the photographs. Quickly, they make their way back through the streets. Drunk children have fallen on the pavement in the poor areas and there is vomit on every street corner. It has been a big day and they will remember it for the rest of their lives. The adults meanwhile are only just getting started. They have paced themselves well. The only drink they are allowed is red wine, but they are making the most of it. Many people will regret it tomorrow, but then tomorrow is the day of the devil.

The two do not speak as they make their way back to the police station. There is something about the incessant beat that is racking the streets which makes speech almost impossible. It makes the city shake and they are glad to get back inside. Immediately, they sit down and open out sandwiches they have bought on the way. Then they sit alone but together in J. D.'s office and start to consider the images. First, they look at the pictures of the women. Quickly that makes them uncomfortable. There are so many, culminating in the seven photographs that scare them the most. Five plain prints of a woman, naked. Then, one print where the dark and light are inverted; an image precisely the same as the others, but cast into a negative. Finally, a last picture of the same woman, her face still obscured, smeared away.

The photographs of the churches, when they consider them, are at first entirely mysterious. All of these images, after all, are of places where they have already been. They are without exception pictures of churches that they have explored the day before. In this final volume, the pictures are throughout lit in negative.

"There's nothing here," J. D. says. "We've been to them all already."

Yawning, he unfolds the translation of the prayer that he made the day before.

"God give us the strength to be weak, to meet brine with blood. God give us the strength to be silent. This is the one prayer and the true prayer. We defy you and we love you, we give ourselves that you give to us, we live that you live and die that you die. We fall that you rise, and rise that you fall. Make a temple to worship God, kill a temple to kill the Lord. This is the prayer of death, to be made in the place of death. This is the prayer of the waters, to be made in the place of waters. This is the prayer to sing to the devil, and this is the prayer to silence him. To turn the waves, we turn the light of the Lord. Change light to dark and dark to light, match each with each and make the devil fall away. To turn the tides, turn only your faith. Amen."

He shrugs.

"Well, we've got that. Turn light to dark. All of them. Every church turned light to dark, and plenty of dead girls to show for it. But they can't all be in on it. They just can't."

As J. D. paces the room, biting the skin on his fingers nervously, Joseph leafs through the negative prints over and over. There is not one church there that they have not visited. Who knows what goes on beneath each church? Who knows what corruption, what agonies? Perhaps one of these negatives shows something... But J. D. is right. They cannot search every church, over and over. Each building is seething with people today, bowing their heads or sneering openly, revelling in the drunken pleasure of being alive. The negative of a church. Change light to dark. He looks at the stained glass windows, the inverted patterns on the gothic arches, the darkness where the light should be. Suddenly, he claps his hands.

"We've been looking in the wrong place."

J. D. looks up with surprise. Joseph is staring at him now, with his eyes a little unfocused as though he is considering empty space.

"Look," he says. "Think about it. The prayer says it all. The pictures say it all. Kill a temple to kill the Lord. Turn light to dark. These photographs aren't supposed to be clear. They are just supposed to show an idea of the right

place to worship, the right place to be. A church that has been killed. Somewhere that's been broken. Somewhere that doesn't worship any more, that's been turned against itself, turned in on itself. We shouldn't be looking in places where people worship, John. We should be looking in places where they don't. We should be looking at places that are *dead*."

With that, he closes the album up, the negative prints turning positive in his thoughts. They need to find any churches that are dead, he thinks. When holiness goes, it leaves a hole in its wake. A hole that has to be filled. Putting on his coat, he gestures for John to do the same. They have to go down to the river. They have to start looking in the dead houses. And they have to do it now.

As they walk from the building, Joseph feels a sense of elation that he has not felt for a long time. He knows where they are going. They are going into the heart of the city. He can hear the rhythm from the radios as he walks down the street, a desperate attempt to start the life of the city again. But the place where the heart used to beat has been dead for years. And when things die, particularly if they are close to water, they quickly begin to go rotten.

As they walk towards the river, their eyes down against the rain, John Douglas cannot help remembering the pictures they have just shared. So many images, and all of them of sacrifice. Somehow he knows, as he walks, that the books of photographs of women will remain unopened for a long time now. They will disappear into the police archives and be opened, perhaps, by some exhausted young man in a decade or two, maybe by someone who is not yet alive. Perhaps he will try to find pleasure in them, but J. D. thinks he won't have much luck. They are far too empty for that.

✝

It is wonderful to kill when you know that you are really bringing rebirth. That is what Peter is thinking, as he walks up and down the church. As he does so, too, he is scuffing

the books onto the ground, destroying the half-neat piles of old library texts that have made little walls in the spaces between the pews. He is very glad now that he piled the books so high, and persuaded the others to do the same. Because of this, almost all of the books are still impeccably dry, and they will burn easily. The church is ruined anyway, he knows. And only two days from now, too, he knows what a miraculous replacement will come. A church of light, a tongue of light, a place of light. A miracle of light. Peter is looking forward to meeting God.

As he walks up and down, Sophia is whimpering slightly, like an animal. None of the others, the men and the women, feel sad about this. In fact, perhaps they are gladdened. Her mouth is gagged and her whimpers are pathetic, but at least they do not sound human and if they only turn their eyes away they can pretend it is a beast who is suffering and afraid, not a Queen. This sacrifice is not like the others and even Rebecca, who from the start was most convinced of the truth of what the librarian has shown them, feels a little uncomfortable. Perhaps it was the need that Peter felt to break Sophia's fingers, one by one. This was a kindness of sorts, he knows that. He was just making sure that she could not sign a contract offered beneath the waves. That she could not work with the devil, but only dance against him. To the others, though, it seemed unnecessarily cruel. Death is one thing, torture quite another.

Because her hands are useless, Peter holds the book in front of her when he asks her to read. He has closed the prayerbook now, and opened again the book of notes and drawings that he has made across the years. There are tears in Sophia's eyes, but those eyes at least are good, and she reads well. Tenderly, now and then, Peter wipes the tears away from her eyes as he turns the pages. She has a lovelier voice by far than Lucia, he thinks. The words were meant for her. He made them only for her, and somewhere deep inside herself she knows it. Her glance flutters over the illustrations, the dark sketches and swirls on the right-hand pages of the book. She reads them quietly, solemnly, in the way they were meant to be read.

When the frightened woman has finished reading the book of notes and drawings, Peter opens once more the book that first told him the truth. He is glad that he does not have to give this book to the girl to hold. For all of her holiness, she is only a young woman and she would not know how to handle books well. He turns past the account of Saint Sophia, her life and death and rebirth from the seas. He reaches beyond all of these, until he arrives at the last page. For this is the page where the prayer is written; the last prayer that the young girl offered up, nine hundred years ago.

"You must be tired," he says to Sophia then. "Not much more now. Everyone, gather round. It's getting late, and we are almost done."

Overcoming their queasiness, the group all stand near to Sophia as she looks at the writing in front of her. Her hands hang useless by her sides, but she is surprised to find she feels little in the way of pain. Sometimes when you have been hurt too much, the pain temporarily stops. Although she cannot quite make herself believe it, too, Sophia is trying to convince herself that this is all only a dream. Perhaps if she acts well she will wake to a new morning. She has been having a lot of nightmares recently and anything is possible. She looks down at the words in front of her. They are in the old language, she sees. The words means nothing to her. At the first word, she stops. Her eyes read it over and over. She cannot bring herself to speak.

After a few moments, Peter smiles.

"Sorry, that was cruel of me," he says. "Just my little joke."

Carefully, he moves the book aside and opens up his own notes again. He turns to the last page.

"I've taken a translation, my dear. Don't worry. The devil speaks all languages. God made them all, you know. Read this version for me. It will make so much more sense to you."

The translation that Peter gives her now is written in verse. The prayer she recites is the same one that J. D. has translated, although the words are slightly different because Peter thinks of himself as a poet. Once, it was written in the

old language. In later centuries, it was turned into Latin, by those who were ashamed of their past. Now it is written out again in language she can understand. Although the poetry is bad, Sophia's nervousness makes it sound holy and her quietness makes it seem intimate, as though she were talking to no-one. As she speaks, she looks up at times at the stained glass window before her. Every time she looks up, Peter tenderly smears the tears away from her eyes, distorting the light from the fires outside.

"God grant us force to have no force, to meet the sea with
blood;
Lord grant us force for silence, grant that silently we cry.
This is the one prayer and the true, Lord grant this
understood.
We love you with the all of us, we love and we defy.
We give ourselves that you give back, we dance against the
flood.
We dance against the devil, and we dance that he may die."

Sophia stops for a moment, her eyes too blurred with tears. With patience, Peter wipes the brine away, thinking only of the rising moon. Slowly, then, he presses one hand against the girl's fingers until she starts to read once more, her voice shivering with fear.

"We fall to calm the waters, and we rise when waters fall,
Make a temple to worship God, with each solemn breath:
Kill a temple, cut a throat, the darker Lord to kill —
This is the prayer of dying, to be made in the place of death.
This is the prayer of waters, to be made where waters spill.
This is the prayer to sing. To turn the waves, turn just your
faith.

This is the prayer to sing to the devil, this is the prayer to say.
Meet light with dark and dark with light, as night is
matched with day:
Match every step the devil makes, to make tides fall away.
Amen."

Immediately after she has finished reciting the poem, Sophia looks up nervously at the man who had translated it. She wants to speak, to tell him it is beautiful. Perhaps to persuade him to let her go. Before she can speak, Peter has reached out towards her.

"No more words," he says.

And with that, he takes a butcher's knife, and cuts away her tongue.

The books are all arranged. Allowing Sophia to live for the moment, the group lead her out of the church. As they do so, Daniel stays behind, with Lucia. She cannot be trusted to join them, of course, and Daniel has a job to do. First, he ties Lucia's hands against one of the pews. She is facing the glass of the window, to keep her calm and fixed on prayer. Quickly then, he takes three cans of petrol and pours them one by one over the books. These are not holy texts. They are completely worthless. There are old romance novels, factual science books that were out of date twenty years ago, the occasional battered bible and historical textbook that is shot through with lies. When he has finished pouring petrol over the driest books, he takes out a bundle of matches from his pocket, bound together with an elastic band. He bends to kiss Lucia on the forehead, and whispers in her ear that she is forgiven all her sins. He must join the others at the river, he says. That is where everything happens. Then, carefully, he walks to the door and strikes one match against the stone. The second that the spark takes hold a line of fire streaks across the floor, flaring up against the books, making the pointless prose blaze light.

Only another day he thinks, and the whole church will rise again. Sophia will rise again. He has felt uncomfortable tonight, seeing the blood spill from her mouth as she tried to keep it closed. He is looking forward, with all of them, to hearing the dear girl speak with a tongue of light. Perhaps Lucia will rise again too. He does not know. Whatever

happens, she has been forgiven and will find a place with God.

Quietly, and calmly, Daniel leaves her now, stepping outside and locking the door to the church as the fire takes hold. As he walks away through deserted streets, he is sad to know that by now he will have missed the sacrifice. But he knows that he, like everyone in this forgotten city, will be there for the resurrection and the light.

It is not as agonising as you might think, being compelled to drown. The terror and the horror come in knowing that it is going to happen. As she is led down roads that are mainly deserted, Sophia is not noticed by anyone who would do anything to help her. The only people in these flood-ravaged streets this late are drunken children, throwing rocks at the windows of long-dead houses, shattering the glass. Only these children see the blood that is pouring from her mouth, if anyone sees it at all. It is difficult to stem blood flowing from such a wound, which is met after all ceaselessly with saliva, freeing up the flow and preventing the cut from healing calmly. The children believe it to be wine. She is drunk, that is why she is staggering. That is why she needs to be supported by her friends.

It is the cusp of midnight when the sacrifice is finally made. It must be made precisely then. The point at which the day of man turns into the day of the devil. They are giving the life of a girl to the devil, they are sealing them together in a pact. They are making the devil dance with the queen, and they have to trick him into thinking it is wholly on his terms. At the very end, as they stand on the near-ruined bridge, Peter and John hold back Sophia's hands as Rebecca gags her one more time. It will of course be easy for the devil to remove the gag from her mouth, but they have to trick him into thinking she can speak and answer his demands. They have to make him think that she is there on his terms. Otherwise he might not dare to dance with her at all.

It is only at this point that Peter takes the seven prayers from the bag where he has kept them, slung across his back. Already they are wrapped in the tin foil that will protect them for the time needed. He burns them carefully around the edges, to make them circular like the moon. Sophia is staggering now and weak as Peter ties the prayers together against her chest, folding her hands over them with the harsh tenderness of a father. When the devil starts to tire, Peter knows, the time will come for sure. God, who will know that Sophia alone is pure, will grant her then a tongue of light. A tongue that can say nothing but good. She will read the prayers to the one who matches her dance. With every prayer, he will weaken more. Seven prayers for seven days. But seven prayers, too, for seven centuries of peace.

For when the devil collapses exhausted, the rising waves will fall away…

At the very end, all four of them kiss Sophia once on each cheek. Peter brushes back her hair. It is thick and dark and lovely and her face is beautifully pale. Carefully, he makes sure that the crown is perfectly in place. Her eyes look tired, he thinks, but the coldness of the water will soon bring new life to them.

"We'll see you soon," he says. "Dance well. Take care. We're relying on you."

Sophia's arms and legs are bound when she is pushed from the bridge. She does not sink at first, however, because she knows that if you breathe in deeply, it is possible to float. Eventually she has to let out her breath, and that is when she drowns.

Chapter Nine.

The storm which approached the city through the night is a great one and it sets everything off kilter for the Day of the Devil, from the start. This was to be a day of flames and fury, but nothing can compete with the lashing rain and nobody wants to. The brief strip of canal that has been annexed off should be covered by petrol at dawn and lit to breathe out flames upon the waters. But when dawn comes, the rain is simply too great. It forces the petrol away, breaking it up into bubbles and patterns. Even if it could be made to rest upon the canal, it would not ignite. The rain falls ceaselessly, and nothing that is not alight already can be lit. Even the fires that are lit already are dying with the ceaseless pressure of the waters. Sick with partying, most people are asleep anyway. Sleep is always the best way to escape a storm.

Lucia, gaining consciousness again, only slowly begins to realise where she is. The river is still rising, the moon only one day away from fullness, and as she sits bound to the front pew of the church she can feel its brutal chill pressing against her upper legs, her waist. Above her, the flames are fighting their own battle with the torture of the storm, and although the roof is burned away at the back, away from the great window, the fire cannot reach the glass and it cannot reach Lucia. Where she expected to be burned, to be torn apart by flames, she finds now that she is only deathly cold. The storm goes on and on, and although there are a few sparks behind her all that is really left of the fire are the ashes of thousands of books, resting upon the surface of the water, pressing against her as she sits there with her hands tied and her mouth sealed shut. She tries to scream but the thunder and the weight of the rain outweigh whatever lonely murmurs she can force from herself. Soon, she starts shivering desperately. Soon after that, the shivering stops. She is glad of this at first, because she imagines she must be

warming with the dawn. But quickly she falls into unconsciousness again, her body very still and her heartbeat patient and slow.

The first people to investigate the last sparks of the dead church are drawn by the swirls of ash they notice on the river. The current is moving very fast and the rain encourages it still more. This is not something that Peter predicted when he let the books burn. The ash has risen on the water and drifted out of the burned-out doors. It has made its way to the canals, and been forced onward by the rain and the tides. Early in the morning, people are already beginning to notice the quickening spill of ash upon the water, soggy burnt paper making patterns. Children follow the ash back to the church, noticing the way that the ash trail is spilling calmly and ceaselessly out of the abandoned building. They are the first to find Lucia, breathing lightly and covered in light that shines in early from the east-facing window, which is good because children can run fast and shout loudly.

The unconscious woman is quickly untied by men in galoshes and greasy coats, and her body is lifted up above the waters. She is placed on a stretcher and carried through the streets. It's slow going, but they reach the nearest hospital eventually. Even here, the water levels are just high enough that the nurses have had to line the doors with sand-bags.

By the time Joseph and John reach the church it is mid-morning and most of the drama has gone. There are still some children, and a couple of adults you wouldn't want to trust. The children all sit on the steps, a little way away from the water. Their faces are, without exception, painted red and when they smile Joseph is alarmed to see that their teeth have been blacked away with dye. Whiteness only shows as sharp slivers, making their teeth seem jagged and brutal. They remain outside the church, however. They are good children, and know that it isn't appropriate to go into

a church made up as the devil, even if this isn't really a church any more.

Because they are good children, too, they know that it is never wise to talk to the police. Both men are now carrying guns, aware of the savagery of the area, and the children mark that as well. They sit silently and stare as the two strangers approach one man, then another. Eventually Joseph sighs and begins to pull out notes from his pocket, with a flick of his wrist. Sometimes you have to make sacrifices. He gives the money to the oldest man there, aware that the very old are often more willing to talk.

"It was something to see."

The man is not made up, but he doesn't need to be. He is hideous, old and thin, and he looks as though he were wearing the skin of a far larger man. His face sags and creases and he is entirely bald and very pale.

"They got her," he says. "I was standing right here. Saw it all. Lovely looking girl, she was. Wouldn't have minded finding her myself. Not that I could have done anything with her. Not at my age." He smiles.

"Took who?"

"How should I know? Don't know anything. Don't tell anything."

Another note. Another smile.

"They fished her out, took her away. Elohim Hospital. She was breathing, I know that much. Out of it. Might still be breathing, for all I know. You should have seen them carrying her. All that paper, floating away."

The rain is still pouring down as Joseph enters the open doors and looks at the charred wreckage of the building. He takes the step down into the building, walking through water. The stained glass window has fractured down the middle and the image of Mary has slumped into the risen river. The wooden pews are still intact, burned at the edges. In the centre of the front row are the remnants of the ropes which tied Lucia. They have been cut abruptly to release her, but the men from the hospital didn't take them away. There are no other police there yet, and this surprises neither of them. Today will be a

busy day for the police, and they can't be everywhere.

Joseph crouches down, looking for fingerprints. There are only two sets here, both those of women. Near the rope, too, he notices that there is more burned paper; old, loose paper that has wholly dissolved into ash.

"Well," he says. "The hospital it is."

Mid-morning, the librarian often likes to be by himself. Now, leaving the others in Daniel's apartment close to the water in the heart of Galata, he makes his way down to the canal alone. He needs his times of silence; he needs his space to think. He has had some of his greatest ideas during these morning times, walking the streets and looking at faces. He loves to look at the statues on the houses by the canal. There are figures there, all of them looking down in penitence, gazing at the waters. Sometimes he feels daunted and bewildered by the magic of them, but today they merely help him strengthen his thoughts. They are all like him, he thinks. Looking down, and waiting. He wonders whether perhaps, when Sophia rises tomorrow, the statues will awaken to welcome her presence. That would be a beautiful thing.

It is difficult to keep secrets and, as Peter walks towards the ocean, he is beginning to feel a little nervous. It is not that he is scared the people of the city will discover him. If they ever do, which he thinks is unlikely, they will discover him after the miracles have happened. They will praise him, love him as a son. But he is scared that his actions will be discovered by someone far stronger than the people of the city. Here, on the day of the devil, he is afraid that somehow, one of the others might let the secret slip. He cannot bear to think what might happen if somebody passes on the secret to the enemy.

It is unfortunate for Rebecca, in the end, that she loves storms so much. She has been told by Peter to stay inside, but she cannot help being drawn out by the thunder. The clouds are heavy with water and as she, too, walks in the

centre of the city she is infatuated by the rapid jags of light that leave sharp imprints in her eyes. The weight of the storm is on the city now, but it is also still blazing over the ocean, so she makes her way out towards the waves. The clouds are so heavy that when she climbs upward she can almost see the lightning reflected in the sea. It is while she is trying to see this that Peter finds her, standing alone.

"Singing to yourself?"

There by the very edge of the ocean, the sea meets with a stone barricade that has stood for centuries. There is no beach, just the wall and then the waves. Some steps lead up the side of the wall, which arcs against the ocean and then yields to permit the canal. Peter stands beside her as she looks out at the furious ocean.

"Peter. I was just…"

"Singing. I know, I heard you. But who were you singing to?"

Rebecca shakes her head. The entire time that she has stood there alone, she hasn't made a sound. She's just listened to the thunder, and thought of Sophia and wondered whether she is really dancing beneath the waves. It all seems a little hard to believe, but she finds it hard to believe too that the ocean could be this furious without good reason.

"I was just looking."

"Ah, you shouldn't feel ashamed. It's good to sing. Provide them with a melody. Something good to dance to. Go on, dear. I'm sure you've got a lovely voice for it."

Rebecca doesn't want to sing, and she says so. She does not feel strong enough to sing for anyone. She is tired and her head hurts a little, and she simply wants to look at the storm and then return to the city, she says. The fact that she refuses to sing for Peter disappoints him, although he does not let her know this. Instead, he stands in silence with the girl, and after a while he smiles at her and shakes his head indulgently and walks away alone.

Just by the ocean, or high up in the suburbs, people have given in entirely to the storm. Nobody is attempting to light flames in those places any more, and if you were a traveller you might be forgiven for thinking today was just an ordinary day in a very quiet place. In the centre of the city, though, people have already begun to devise ways of evading the storm. The main streets cannot be sheltered, because they are too great, but here in the heart there are plenty of thin alleys; low streets of stone houses that have slumped together for centuries. Unskilfully but very quickly, wooden lattices have been slung across these alleyways.

Fires have been lit in the middle of the roads, and flames have taken hold.

These alleys are very crowded now. People from all around the city have heard that the flames that were to blaze on the waters and in the main square have been shifted here, and they have brought their past to burn. Anything they don't like, or don't want; photographs of lovers they have since learned to loathe, or last year's clothes or school textbooks. Tax returns from years ago and boring books and unfashionable records. It's all to go to the devil. The mound of once-loved garbage is growing greater in the road. Beside it, passive figures dressed in black rake away the ashes and put them in rubbish bags. The roads must be kept empty enough to support the blaze.

Daniel's apartment is on one of these alleys, on the second floor. Now, Peter is standing with the others, looking out. Above them, the sky is completely kept away by the wooden slats, while below them flames are flickering. Occasionally, playfully, someone in the street throws something from a window. People walk past beside the flames, but none of them are ever Rebecca.

Joseph has nothing to burn, but as he hurries through the crowd on his way to the hospital he can feel a nervous tension in his stomach. He feels pathetic because he doesn't

even have a past that he thinks is worth burning. All his old photographs went ages ago, shortly after his old life fell apart. He threw them into the water. He didn't burn them. He had hoped they would spill away in the river, floating on the surface gracefully, but that hadn't happened. They had clumped together and fallen away very rapidly, and then there had been nothing but the birds. Her dresses had gone earlier; he had given them back to her mother.

The narrow, covered roads are the quickest way to the hospital, but they are so busy with people that soon the pair of them begin to take a different route. Now they are walking along a wider road where nobody and nothing is. The sounds of the crowd can be heard from a vast distance, and even when they are far away they don't sound natural. There are women wailing absurdly, sounding like Spanish widows, screaming out their imagined grief.

When they reach the hospital, Joseph and J. D. quickly see that it is the only place in the city that has retained some sort of sanity and clarity. The walls are clean and the ambulances are neatly parked outside. Walking inside, they quickly ask to see the victim and are taken to her. She is unconscious but her breathing is deep and calm. Standing beside her, wrapped up in her own thoughts, Rebecca is gazing down at the girl and thinking to herself. She has only just arrived herself, and is still drenched with the rain. Unthinkingly, Joseph falls into the role of good cop, fetching her a towel and smiling with concern.

"You know her?" he asks, tenderly.

Rebecca looks at him with terror but still takes the towel, drying first her face and then her hair, which hangs lank and dark about her face.

"I didn't want anything bad to happen to her," she says. "She will be alright."

It isn't a question, just a statement.

"Maybe," says Joseph.

"No, she will. Everything will be alright tomorrow."

"Were you friends?"

"I was helping her out, yes. We helped each other."

"Well, that's what friends do, isn't it?"

Rebecca looks up at him, and then at J. D. kneeling down at the bedside. Suddenly she is very tired, and wants nothing more than for tomorrow to come. Carefully, well aware that the moment has arrived, Joseph puts one arm around the girl and holds her close until she begins to cry. At last, he thinks, they are really getting somewhere.

They stay there together for fifteen minutes, but Rebecca says nothing else throughout that time. Although she would not say she cared about this girl, the presence of the police suddenly make this real in a way that it has never been before. The hospital is clear and clean, and apart from the occasional victim of the festivities it is completely removed from the wildness of the rest of the city. She is still drunk on the wine that she had been drinking alone by the ocean, and eventually the fact that the alcohol is wearing off makes her feel as though everything else is wearing off too; as though the whole of the week has been nothing more than a dream. Joseph holds her close to him and gently, over and over, repeats the same words.

"It's over now," he says. "It's over now."

Eventually, she allows herself to believe him, and that is when she begins to talk.

Chapter Ten.

The rain was washing away the shadows outside when the librarian finally realised that Rebecca was not coming back. It was not that anyone told him; it was simply an increasing awareness, unspoken among the three of them. She has gone, and he is not surprised. As he stands there looking down at the tongues of flame, though, he quickly realises that he has to leave Daniel's apartment. He has to leave everywhere that is familiar. Until they can find Rebecca – until they are sure that she has not gone to the other side. They have to leave anywhere that they could be found.

It is time to leave by then anyway, and he does not feel sad to be leaving. He has everything that he needs. Carefully, he tells Daniel and John that they should search the city for Rebecca. If they feel that the police might find them, he says, they should make their way out of the city, get as far away as possible. They will know when it is time to return, he says. They will see by the blinding light. He watches them as they walk out towards the outskirts of the city, together, but he turns and goes the other way alone.

By now the rain is starting to abate but it is still busy in the gutters, and as he walks along with his head down that is the most beautiful thing; the way in which the flames reflect in running water, spinning and turning and gathering and burning, running down the sides of the road in tender rivulets of light. It is dusk and the firelight can only grow stronger. Looking up, Peter is delighted to see that the full moon is beginning to break through the clouds. The storm, which came in from the sea, is moving up to the hills and while there are occasional whiplashes of lightning the rain will be nothing very soon.

Although it is not a safe place to be in one way, in another the centre is the safest place to stay. It is the place where everyone is, and when a place is wholly crowded all of the people there become faceless and unrecognisable. He

has another reason to go into the centre, as well. He has always said that he would light a candle, and he has always known that he must.

The tradition of the night demands it, and Peter is a stickler for tradition. Already as he grows closer to the main square and to the river beside it he can see the market traders selling their little tin candles, laid out on trays and very cheap. When he reaches the centre, he sees that they are everywhere and the sight is staggering. All of the streetlights have been switched off in the central square. The great fires that have overwhelmed the little streets are non-existent here. In their place are rows and rows of little candles, waiting to be sold. He buys one for his mother and he takes it down to the river.

Here, there are barges already, waiting. Because the rain has gone now the ceremonies have returned to the way that they should be, all exposed flame flickering in the breeze. Some of the barges already have candles on and Peter adds his own, then stands and waits. Today there is nothing to do but wait, and wonder, and breathe in the horror and the glory and the dampness on the air.

Peter arrives at the river at eight at night, and stands there watching the people change. The children, with their ugly fury, are slowly taken away; their places filled by adults whose anger and sadness are more orderly. At ten, when the air is very cold and the lightning on the hills has wholly fallen away, the barges suddenly begin to fill more and more rapidly with lit candles. By eleven there are seven barges there on the river, one for each of the days of the week, and every one completely filled with little tin-and-wax candles, their quick flames shivering in the chill.

It is at eleven that people start to show their grief more fully than they have before. While throughout the day there have been occasional wails of sorrow, brief laments by women burning pictures, now the sadness is deeper, more desperate and more sincere. The candles that they have placed upon the barges are pressing and flickering against each other, every one representing another soul. People know that it is tradition to light the candles today of all

days; to set the barges free and send the souls out to the sea. But very few of them, Peter knows, understand precisely why.

This late, there are no children around apart from those with no one to care for them. These run through the crowds, young and furious. People of all ages are painted like devils, and that makes Peter feel a little afraid. The people are mocking tradition; they are laughing at the notion of the devil, even as they light the candles and prepare to set the barges loose. Looking down at the muscular water, the way that the tendons of the waves press and pull, he wonders to himself that anyone can think that this is something to laugh about. But although they are painted like devils, dancing like demons, carrying flaming torches and allowing the fires to touch and connect and ignite new flames from the old, he knows deep within that, at least, the true and necessary custom is being maintained. The tradition that has been maintained ever since the time of Saint Sophia and the miracle of the waves…

Every hundred years, they send them down. The barges filled with flames, the candles to represent souls. The idea is that they are sending candles to represent the souls of those they love, and who have gone. But that's not the truth. Peter knows what the truth is. To dance this greatest dance, Sophia needs light.

Peter stands alone through everything. At certain times, people try to coax him into a dance. It is a complex dance, in that it tries to maintain the rhythm of the waves. No one knows why this must be; they simply know that it must. Now, the sea has reached its greatest height, and this close to the river the dance takes place ankle-deep in water. Tonight, the night that connects the Day of the Devil with the Day of God, the moon is full and very low. Light threads through the clouds, which are thinning into nothing, and the stars pin the darkness in place.

He will not dance.

He will only look and ensure that duty is done to Sophia.

It would be awful to try to dance with the devil in darkness.

Although by midnight most people are very drunk, and possessed of the sad fury that comes with a drunken lament, Peter is pleased and relieved to see that this does not affect their timekeeping. Sophia needs all the light she can have, tonight, to keep up the dance and to follow the steps of her partner. At twelve exactly, the great bells begin to ring in the central square. Their sound, normally muffled at night, dominates the dark until even the rivers seem to shiver with their resonance. And then, on the very last note of the bell, at the precise moment when the Day of the Devil slips away into the Day of God, the ropes are cut, and – taken solely on the flow of the river itself – the barges slip away.

Peter stands there and watches them move. All around him, people are clapping their hands with the rhythm of the waves, slowly and heavily. Smoke fills the air and stings his eyes until they ache with almost-tears. The barges move calmly through the harbour. It is wonderful to watch. They are steered by no one, but the water takes them delightedly, steering them as a mother guides her children.

The river itself is quiet, protected a little. The barges jostle and press and make their way through the water. Soon, however, they start to be affected by the force of the waves at the mouth, where the river meets the sea. Peter does not move from where he is standing, preferring to watch from a distance. He knows there will be crowds there, standing at the harbour's edge. As he stands there, he sees it happen and for the first time in months he begins to feel calm. Everything is working according to plan. There, far away, he sees the first barge get taken by the waves. He imagines it rocking, pressing, taken out by the high tide.

Soon, all of the barges are out there on the sea. They are sturdy, and they will not sink, albeit that the waves are strong. They will simply float and drift together, there on the surface of the sea. And the light that they carry and the love that they carry, Peter knows, will shine downwards through the darkness. It will break through the surface of the sea, and it will dazzle the depths and it will mean that sweet Sophia can see the dance that the devil is making, and can match him, step for step.

Be strong, he thinks, as he watches the candles burning together in the distance.

Our hopes are in you.

As Peter stands there, he listens to the clapping of thousands of hands, in time with the pressure of the waves. He thinks he has never heard anything more beautiful. And though he is shy, and is scared of the crowd, he is proud of the part he has played. Slowly, almost without thinking, he finds himself clapping in time with the sea and the crowd.

He knows he will never feel part of something as great or as honest again.

Chapter Eleven.

When the rain has begun to dissipate, around four that morning, the gulls begin to swirl and gather. The day will not begin for hours, but perhaps they are deluded by the weight of the full moon, which is pressing down fully now upon the sea and the land. They are very awake, and their screams wake up others. Children, lying in bed, try to twist these cries in their ears and make them sound like something jubilant. Today should be a celebration, but in honest truth the sounds are horrible, agitated and sharp.

The moon is a wonderful help to the fishermen, who are confident of a good haul tonight. They cast their wide nets across the ocean, used to the screaming gulls, which hang low and hope to parasite on their catch. Mostly their catch is good and they watch the fish leaping and writhing in their nets and smile to each other, and some even take photographs because today will not happen again, and others throw some of their dead load to the birds. Eventually the fishers make their way in to land again and the sun begins to come up. When it does so it illuminates an exhausted city. Although this should be a day of celebration, the streets still echo with the weak dregs of the drunkenness that possessed it.

At dawn there are still four barges milling around just outside the harbour, lifting and dropping on the dull, numbing waves. That the candles on these remaining barges, the only ones that will be found now, have all gone out is immediately evident to the fishermen who see them and pass them. They chart the positions of the barges and they hand those details in to the proper authorities, the marine police that guard and protect the immediate territory. Immediately the authorities send out chartered tugs with strong engines, which drag the boats back into the harbour, where they will be strapped under netting for later use. The wax will be stripped from them completely fairly

131

soon, and they are to be sent out again to serve more normal, practical tasks. It is never good to waste, when waste is not necessary.

Very few people see any of this happen, because most people are asleep and those who are not are watching the final flickering of flames in the city centre and thinking about the future or the past. Joseph and J. D. are still awake, although Rebecca is sleeping now. She has cried herself out but she has told them everything she knows about the librarian and the sacrifices. She is comfortable in a single room in the hospital, although when she wakes up she will find that the door has been firmly locked. Lucia is still unconscious, her mind drifting somewhere out of reach.

As Joseph and J. D. walk towards the great city library together they are shivering in the thin winter sunlight. Graffiti streaks everything, everywhere. Dedications of love are the main theme; dedications of hate are the next. There is only one recurrent picture, which is always painted in red. It's simple and uniform, because all of the pictures were painted using spray-paints and cheap stencils that many people bought the night before. The images are of a leering face, smiling and angry. Sharp horns curl from its head. Mostly the picture is painted on glass; shop fronts or the windows of houses. The eyes are hollow, but where the lights inside are turned on, they shine against this early, chilly light.

When they reach the library, the two are not surprised to see that the painters have been here too. They have taken in every municipal building and there was no reason to suppose here should be an exception. The two tap the glass from the outside as they approach the doors, which are surprisingly unmarked and unsurprisingly locked. The doors are locked, however, in a weak and easily broken way – the thin latch nothing that they can't break down. When they have cracked the hinges they pause for a moment and J. D. reaches into his right hand pocket and passes Joseph a pistol which is dark with no recognisable maker's mark, just in case. And then, they force their way in to the main library and immediately turn on the lights.

"It hardly looks like a murder scene."

The library has been closed throughout the day of man and the day of the devil and it looks like a place from the past. The books are all immaculately ordered. In the newspaper stands, the newspapers from the forgotten day are still standing straight upright, their banners and blankness a symbol from a time of calm forgetfulness. Slowly, the two make their way down the centre, looking warily down the alphabeticised aisles. Joseph's hand is firmly on his gun and he wonders if he would shoot if he were forced to, as he always used to wonder. The doors were firmly locked, but when you are walking like this you wonder about ghosts, and you remember that people can get in and stay in, regardless of whether the front door is padlocked. But there is no one to be seen.

The metal door, when they reach it, is of course locked but they know enough to switch the power off. The second they switch it off, thin light streams through the windows with new force and lights the place up like a cathedral. Joseph opens the door fast then, with J. D. a little behind. Perhaps he is warier because he has a child. Joseph would like to say that he has no qualms, but he feels a stitch in his side although he has no physical reason to, and his heart is beating relentlessly.

Inside the inner, windowless room, the ancient manuscripts still stand upright and protected by thin plastic sheets. The account of Thomas Burthen means far less to Joseph and J. D. than it meant to Lucia or Peter. They only see that it is an old sheet of manuscript, elegantly written but brutal in intent. Joseph reads the writing briefly: *For She was the Saint of Life and Death, and She was Saint Sophia.* J. D. however has not been drawn to the manuscripts. On the dry wooden table, scattered out but vaguely arranged according to date, he sees newspaper accounts and he remembers what he was told when he was training, years ago. Sometimes, newspapers tells the truth before it even happens.

Peter has been as meticulous as any man could be. The newspapers from one hundred years ago are there – the

papers that J. D. assembled, and more. There are sketches of the murder victims, in the cheaper papers; hurried drawings by skilled but harried artists, working against time with no real idea of what the dead girls looked like. The words describe the deaths that he has already read of, and he only looks through them hurriedly. It's enough to confirm what he thought long ago, and the silence of the room is enough to confirm that the librarian is far away.

When Joseph has glanced at the manuscript, he notices that there is one corner of the room where the meticulous cleanliness falls away. Here, a bundle of recent newspapers have been bunched together in a vast heap with dates that span several months. Their headlines at first seem worth nothing at all, simply dramatic accounts of the waters that are taking over the city, couched in hysterical terms. But as he moves his way through all the papers, he becomes aware of one thing. Every headline, every paper, contains one word. Rising. Soon, he has reached beyond the newspapers, to discover something else. There, beneath everything, is a mass of photocopied papers. They are scattered together, bound in groups by elastic bands. All of them are precisely the same, and each one of them is a prayer with the same words. Some of them, he has never read before, but some of them he recognises – Water, Sun and Hope. And underneath everything, making a sort of nest for the prayers, there is a pile of women's clothing. Alongside this are a few locks of hair. These are only little curls like lover's mementos, and every one has been carefully tied with a thin piece of silver wire.

The dawn rises on the sea. Before dawn, Peter has already climbed high up on the hill, to the wall where the old city ends and the new city spills out. He wants to be the first person in the old part of the city to greet this new dawn, because he feels within his soul that something miraculous will happen. The moment that the sunlight touches the wall, he has read, is when it will occur. She will rise from

the sea with the sunlight. She will rise singing sweetly with a tongue of dry light. As he stands there at the edge of the city, with his back pressed against the ancient wall, his heart is thumping in numb agitation. There are clouds, and he curses that. He was looking forward to the way that the sunlight would spill across the streets. Sophia, after all, must sing with sunlight. But surely she will have the strength to force away the clouds.

This near the winter solstice, sunrise lasts forever. On a cloudy day, in particular, it is impossible to precisely tell where night ends and day begins. As he stands waiting for the dawn, Peter thinks about how he can measure the moment. How can we ever measure a moment where something becomes something else? When does a baby receive its soul when it breaks out into the world? He has the precise time of the sunrise, the scientific time, written in his mind. He has all the details. Dawn must officially break a little past eight. Peter waits and sees the way that the first hints of sunlight behind the heavy cloud are creating a nest for the dawn. Calmly, he sings a few hymns to himself, nothing compared to what he knows will come. Half past seven turns to eight, and the air all around him seems to flutter with a breeze that goes every which way and does not settle. The wall behind him is marked over and over with the hollow-eyed stencil painting of the devil. Everyone else is asleep, or still in the centre of the city, drunk and unaware of what must happen. Only Peter is here, giddy with excitement.

Immediately before dawn, he senses it. The warmth rises, blowing in from the sea. He sings the same hymn again and again now, in a voice that is raised and agitated. Briefly, he falls back against the wall, his spirit soaring in rapture. The sun is rising now – it has to be. It is pressing against the clouds, leading his princess to the surface. She will be tired, but she will be joyous. Soon, he will see his old friends again. They will thank him for finding a way back. His friends who died before their time will live again. But more than that, the dead who have suffered beneath the sea so long will be free. All of the sinners from

the city, all of those dead souls trapped under the water, lost in darkness.

Peter imagines the souls rising up into heaven; how they will be met there by a god who is all-forgiving. He imagines the waters surging backwards from the centre of the city, the stone-eating brine moving away towards the sea. He sees how the devil has been danced into exhaustion; how he will stop the waves from rising now. There is no way that the devil can keep up the dance any longer, he thinks. A new saint is born today, or an old saint reborn.

Saint Sophia has come again, rising with the dawn.

Joyous, desperate with anticipation, Peter looks out at the streets that are starting to receive the winter sunlight. He listens to the everyday sounds of the waking city, and waits to hear the music start beneath the familiar bustle. He waits and waits in the cold new light.

He waits, and nothing happens.

Down below, the barges are being guided home. The lights on them are dead. Slowly, throughout the wrecked city, people are beginning to turn on their radios and televisions. As Peter stands with his back against the wall, he holds his hands high and stares at the thin brightening in cloud that shows the place of the weary winter sun. It is barely noticeable. It is very cold now and a light rain is beginning to fall, feeble in comparison with the harsh storms that have pressed and twisted light for so long. Peter lifts his eyes up to the sky, but for once they are not raised in prayer. Instead, he looks upward to try to stem the tears that he can feel gathering. As the minutes go by and strangers walk past, he feels the wild exhilaration start to fall away. He is tired in the bones, and his straightened hands ache as he presses his fingers up towards the sky.

Peter leaves the city wall a little after nine. Although his hopes have faded to almost nothing, he tries to hold on to his faith as he walks back down into the city. With every step he takes, he sees more stencils of the devil. He walks

through the narrow streets, which all slope slightly down towards the sea. It seems as though the eyes of the pictures follow him as he goes, and although he clings to the desperate belief that the seas are starting to recede, he is unsurprised in truth to find that, when he gets to Gowyim street, the first fluttering of the sea remains there. Walking through the shallow waters, he pauses a moment to take off his shoes, which he leaves in a shop doorway. It is beautiful to walk in the waters, although it means he has failed.

As he walks barefoot down Gowyim street, Peter soon begins to see the stalls that have stood throughout the city all through the festival. Desperate profiteers have waited here day by day, selling what goods they could, making money. Mostly they have been foreigners who have swept in to clean the cash away from this dying city. Today, Peter sees, all of their wares are cut-price. There would be no point taking them away from the festival, after all, and the people are trying to make as much as they can while the going is still almost good.

"Mask of the devil? Souvenir? Souvenir, sir… Please, sir."

A child with blue eyes and fair hair and broken teeth looks up, smiling at him. He walks past, ignoring the request. As he moves on, he notices one drunk man locked in an argument with another. Both are holding bottles of wine, but one is clearly begging.

"Give me something for nothing, mister? In honour of the day of forgetting?"

A man with a hung-over look glances down at the beggar as he pleads for more wine-money, and shakes his head.

"It's over."

Peter stands and listens to the brief exchange.

It's over.

Peter reaches the library just a little later than Joseph and J. D. but he does not try to go in. He can see from a distance that the doors have been unlocked and that it is no longer a safe place. For a moment he stands there and thinks of the curls of hair from all the beautiful women, and wonders at the fact that those are all that is left of the women now. He can't understand what he has done wrong.

If the library was safe, he thinks, he might go in and look. He might read the papers again, think about the manuscripts, try to find some kind of forgiveness in the ancient words. There must be some way that he can save the situation, save Sophia and the city. He can't bear to think of her trapped down there and dancing for evermore.

After he has stood there for a little while, watching the doors from a distance, the librarian turns and walks down further towards the sea. The full moon has kept the waves ridiculously high, but people still have to earn a living, so the street traders are still standing secure in their positions. Here where the waters are so high, most shops have closed, but the newspaper men who work on the streets have their papers on tables high above the ankle-deep water. Although he desperately wants to be, Peter finds he is not even surprised when he sees the main headline that the men are calling out.

Another body has been washed up, a girl without a tongue.

The body of Sophia was washed up early that morning, early enough to make the second printing of the papers. The man who found her claimed her crown had been washed away, but he was not a man to be trusted about that. He kept it, because it was beautiful, and later perhaps when all this was forgotten he gave it to his own girl.

The body itself was naked and all of its muscles were stiff by then. The man who found it thought for a while of hiding it, or slinging it back in the river, so that he did not have to lie about keeping the silver for himself. He knew from the first who she was. He'd been in the square when she'd given her talk, and he knew that whoever found her would be under some sort of suspicion. Quickly, guilt overcame him because he was not a bad man, and drunkenly he walked away from the river and up to a main street where he told other men. In a group, they walked down to where the body lay, and stood and stared for a while.

"For God's sake," one of them said after a while. "Cover her up, someone."

The old man who had spoken removed his jumper, to wrap around her. Another bound a shirt against her legs, to protect her modesty. Finally, they cleaned the last of the blood away from her face; the blood that not even the sea had washed fully away. Then eventually, almost instinctively, a woman who was with them telephoned for an ambulance, as though she thought the water-cold girl could be hauled somehow back from the dead.

Ordinarily, perhaps, ambulance-men would resent being called out to drag away the dead. It's not their job to come racing through the streets to save corpses, after all, and it's hard to move against the water anyway. They had to park their ambulance far from the river, and come rushing in by foot. But this was Sophia, of course, and on this day of all days no one could really deny her anything. And so they put her body on a stretcher, which they carried through the waterlogged streets until they reached the ambulance itself. On her final journey to the hospital, the driver drove fast and the sirens screamed out.

By mid-morning almost everyone in the city knows what has happened. There is a sense of bewilderment and of numbness throughout. No one knows precisely what to do. A celebration has been arranged, they know that much. In the central square, the bishop who started this all was to introduce the girl who represented the city once again. She was due to give a beautiful speech, in praise of their dying home. And so, although they know that of course Sophia will not be there, almost everyone in the city gravitates towards the centre nonetheless. The great wooden podium has been erected in preparation for the speech of Sophia, and people gather and stand and stare and wait. Peter too makes his way towards the square and stands there with the others. He stands at the back, allowing the children and women to stand in front of him. He can see perfectly well

from the back, after all. At mid-day precisely, Joseph and J. D. are standing in the hospital gazing at the dead body of the beautiful girl. Peter, meanwhile, is standing with the others in Elohim, looking up at the podium where the bishop is waiting despondently to make his final speech.

"This is a day of sorrow," the bishop says mournfully. His voice, normally strong, is weak in the winter breeze. "But let us not forget that it is also a day of joy. Let us not forget that this has been a week of celebration. Although we mourn a death, today must be a celebration of life." He looks out. In front of him stands almost everyone in the city, crammed together in the square. Peter touches the stone of the building behind him as he listens.

"Let us not forget," the bishop says, "that while the heart of a single person still beats in this city, the city lives on. Let us not forget."

Slowly, then, he starts to clap his hands. Although this was not arranged before, although none of this could have been arranged, the people in the crowd quickly understand the meaning of this gesture. The hands that clap symbolise the heartbeat of the city, a pulse that has not died and will not die. Women guide their children as the rhythm begins. Rapidly, the noise moves through the square, growing with each second. In the streets beside the square, people who have arrived late stand stunned and listening to the rhythm. They are too far away to have heard the speech, but they too understand. Very quickly, together, the people of Galata begin to clap their hands with a slow, calm beat.

Peter stands at the very back, and he alone does not clap his hands. The water is cold against his bare feet. Awkwardly, he moves through the crowd and out through one of the narrow streets. As he makes his way towards the river, he can hear the clapping of thousands of people. All through the streets, the crowds block his path, and even when he finally escapes from the throng he can hear the pulse of the city behind him, ceaseless as he makes his calm way down towards the river.

Chapter Twelve.

The body of Sophia is not pretty, although Joseph tries to make it better by closing her eyes. The only pretty thing about it, he thinks, is his own hope that it will be the last, at least for this case. Rebecca has told them almost everything about the past; the sacrifices of young women through the days. While she was less than willing to confess everything at first, claiming that the dead gave their lives willingly, she is as aware as anyone that the spell has not worked. She realised it at dawn, when the shallow seas continued to shiver their way through the streets. Young, unattractive and cold even after hours in the warm closed hospital room, Rebecca feels a little as though she has risen from a dream. It is like rising alive from the depths of a savage ocean, she thinks, but of course that cannot happen.

Although Rebecca swears at first that the sacrifices were willing and necessary, young women who had chosen to die even if the spell has failed, by noon one thing has changed her mind. It is not made public knowledge at first, although the newspapers will publish it in the end. They are well mannered enough to wait, however, to see whether the mother of the dead baby can be found. A tiny child, washed up with the tide, barely recognisable as anything much after so many days in the sea. Joseph tells Rebecca the news as soon as he is told himself, offering the bewildered girl coffee and assuring her it is not her fault and she will not be blamed. As he observes to her drily, however, she had not mentioned that a baby had died. She had said nothing about that.

Rebecca stares at him for a moment before she speaks again, and when she does she picks her words very carefully, aware she is being confronted with the truth and conscious that if she is not honest now, things will go badly for her.

"There was a baby," she says. "Yes, there was. But he said

she would go back." The plain girl shivers there, looking for forgiveness in Joseph's empty eyes. "It wasn't meant, I'm sure. He wouldn't do that. He's not like that, not Peter. He said she'd go back to her mother."

The discovery of the child changes the case for Joseph. He asks not to see the child's body, but he cannot stop thinking about it. The others, he thinks, did not know what they were doing, but they should have realised. And while the women had not wished to die themselves, almost all of them were willing to let others die for the sake of a spell. The baby had been innocent. As Rebecca said herself, that was supposed to be the point.

Joseph reached a point long ago when he stopped caring about most deaths. But it is impossible for him not to care about the death of someone wholly innocent, and he sits alone with Rebecca for some time, trying to be kind to her and hating her for her part in it. He knows he should be working on the case; that the murderer is still out there somewhere. For some time, however, he cannot move and he can hardly breathe. Joseph is exhausted and simply wants someone else to take over the case.

After he told Rebecca that she will not be blamed, Joseph seemed to forget how to speak for a while. He sat motionless, exhausted. Perhaps he would have stayed still for hours, if J. D. hadn't entered the cool white room silently behind him with the only news that might have stirred him back to life.

Lucia has woken up.

Joseph stays with Lucia for hardly any time, but that is enough to fire him into fury once more. While she is conscious, she is still a little bewildered, crying and confused. At first she makes hardly any sense, but soon she is talking to the two of them about the way that Daniel spoke to her as he covered the books with petrol. How she sat there, her mouth taped closed, and listened as the man solemnly listed the plans of the group. The way in which he

looked at her with a glance that was something like love, and then told her he was leaving to join the others at Oerim Bridge. That's the last thing she remembers, she says.

Everything happens down at the river.

If Joseph were being responsible, now would be the time to tell others what to do. He is exhausted and he is not even a member of the police any more. It's not his business, and there seems to be nothing more to discover. Everything happens down at the river. He should just pass that information on, and go home. As he stands there with J. D. listening to the tearful account of the girl, however, he is grateful to see that the other man, too, seems eager to let no one else take the glory for this case. The death of the child has changed everything. The two don't want Peter to be brought to justice. They want to see the bastard die. Carefully, Joseph stands up, his arm a little sore in the damp air. The two of them tell Lucia that they'll be back, and they thank the nurses who are watching over her. As they leave the hospital with a hurried walk, Joseph feels for the holster at his side. Although the gun has not been fired, it feels oddly warm, as he slips off its safety-catch so that he can be ready.

The crowds make moving through the city difficult for Peter, but he is in no real hurry. He weaves slowly against the tide of people, pressing onward. The risen water gets no higher, because the city here this close to the river is built on a level. He strides through the water and feels it swell and press against his bare feet. The sacrifices have come to nothing, he thinks. There is nothing else for it now. If the girls were not strong enough to win the fight, Peter must confront the devil himself. Perhaps he can win. That is his only hope.

As he walks through the city with his feet bare, there is something spiritual about Peter. His eyes shine and his head is raised slightly, as though he were completely ignorant of the cool dirty water that chills against his feet. It is getting

later now, a little after four, and darkness is beginning to move in against the town. The clapping is starting to die down, as the stars flick on one by one. Soon, the sun has gone and Peter finds himself guided only by the moon, which guides the tide.

The route that Peter takes to the river is not the straightest one. He needs to say goodbye to places first. He cannot go to the library. He knows that much, and it makes him sad. But he needs to get one thing before he can make his way to the river. He needs to get hold of a knife. Walking calmly through the streets, he makes his way back to the foreign part of the city. He glances at Ezekiel's shop as he walks past, but the old man is out with so many of them, down at the square. A little way on, he goes into an old store with paper over its windows. The inside is quite dark, and too many of the knives are not the sort that Peter wants. There are flick-knives, shiny-bright children's toys, he thinks. In truth, he did not need to go into such a shop to buy the knife he finally chooses, which hangs from a hook pointing downward. It is only an old-fashioned butcher's knife, after all. Sometimes simplicity is best.

When he leaves the shop, Peter's heart is heavy with fear for the first time. He has to be strong, he thinks, stronger than he has ever been. He sees it now. It was wrong of him to try to make others do the job. Some things you simply have to do yourself.

Although Joseph and J. D. walk a straighter path to the river they also move slowly, held back by the people everywhere. The hardest to walk past are the children, who press against their legs and sometimes beg. While the adults are mournful now and solemn, most children past a certain age are trying furiously to celebrate still. They are all aware that this is the last day of the festival, and while they have been told that now is a time to be sad, they have been determined to celebrate for days. A death means very little to them, when they have prepared themselves for so long.

They enjoyed the clapping, and now they are enjoying getting drunk.

After a little while the two men decide to turn down a narrow side street, which is less crowded. They make a faster pace then, and soon reach a canal that will lead to the river itself. While the bank of the canal is covered with water, the main body of the water remains fully visible. They walk through water along the narrow stone path. The lights have turned on in many of the houses now, illuminating bouquets of flowers that many have put in their windows, either for mourning or for celebration. There are very few people outside here, and none of them try to get in the way of the pair. This is a respectable part of the city, and J. D.'s uniform is recognised and feared.

Eventually the pair walk through the respectable streets and the roads begin to become more dirty. The canal here is filthy, with rubbish bags floating on its surface. They move away from the centre and towards the mouth of the river, where the less reputable and more decayed parts of the city stand waiting to fall into the sea. The two pass Elohim bridge, then Aisha bridge, where two lovers are kissing, leaning against a light. Eventually, in the distance, they see it. The oldest bridge in the city and the nearest to the sea. Children are singing in the distance, somewhere, their song surprisingly innocent and simple. But directly in front of them, Gowyim Bridge stands still and waiting, lit by flaming torches that have been tied to posts across the water.

When he has bought the knife, Peter makes his own way straight to Gowyim Bridge. It is the bridge nearest the sea, and the sacrifice will be better made here. All the way to the bridge he has been thinking about how it will be. He knows how to cut skin and how to break bone. He has rubbed the edge of the knife over his fingertips as he has walked through the streets. There is no way that Peter could be more prepared for what must happen. As he reaches the

bridge, the children in the distance have already started singing. It is time to act. With a matter-of-fact smile that even he cannot convince himself is spiritual, the librarian pulls out the knife and runs it one more time against his skin. Carefully, he rolls up his sleeves. Then, with one movement, he brings the knife down against his flesh. He makes small cuts, not enough to kill himself yet, just enough to weaken. He must be sure that he will not be able to swim back to the surface. Peter does not trust himself.

By the time that he sees the others in the distance, Peter has already covered his arms with little cuts. The air has begun to seem thinner, and he has started to feel giddy. He wants to be able to swim to the bottom. He knows he must be strong enough for that. But he must be weak enough not to be able to return. By the time that they see him, he is already almost in another world, looking first at the flames and then at their reflections in the water. He thinks of the devil waiting, as he looks at the reflected light. It is as though it is burning down there.

Joseph recognises the librarian first. One man, standing with his head bowed on the water's edge. Although they are some distance away, his first instinct is to shoot. Instead, at J. D.'s quiet insistence, he holds back. The moon is rising a little way above, and perhaps it is that as well that compels him to stay calm.

"Wait there," he says. "Police. Don't move."

Neither he nor J. D. is running. The water prevents it, and their wariness. Carefully, they walk closer to the bridge, so close that they can smell the smoke from the flaming torches and see the light reflected in the lone man's eyes.

"Don't move," he says again. "I'm warning you."

"Or what?"

The librarian is looking at them with a very peaceful expression, standing in the middle of the bridge. Carefully, as they watch him from the edge, he lifts up his hands as though he is making a show of surrender. The knife shines brightly in his right hand. Joseph angles his gun at the man.

"Or I'll kill you."

Peter smiles, then shrugs. The day has come but the tides

have not fallen away. He looks at the guns of the two men, standing only twenty paces away. He wonders how good they are with the weapons. His head is spinning so much, he finds, that he doesn't even care.

"I'd hate to cause you the bother," he says.

With the infinite carefulness of a man made drunk by the loss of too much blood, then, he presses the knife against his tongue and cuts it clean away. He does so with such speed that the others are afraid he may be reaching for a gun. Because of this, at the precise moment when he feels his own tongue fall away within his mouth, Peter hears the sound of the first of many shots.

Peter is bleeding to death when he falls into the water. The shots have hit him, one in the arm and another in the stomach. He finds, though, that he is still able to put his hands together in a kind of prayer, and when he is underwater he is even able to swim a little while into the deep. J. D. stops shooting the moment he is underwater, but Joseph wastes bullet after bullet firing into the tidal river, there at the point where it just becomes the sea. Eventually the two men turn away, and make their way back to the city. As for Peter, in the place where he is going there is nothing, or maybe just light.

Acknowledgements

Thanks to Louise Willder for a critical reading of the text and her encouragement of my writing endeavours.

Elsewhen Press

delivering outstanding new talents in speculative fiction

Visit the Elsewhen Press website at elsewhen.press for the latest information on all of our titles, authors and events; to read our blog; find out where to buy our books and ebooks; or to place an order.

Sign up for the Elsewhen Press InFlight Newsletter at elsewhen.press/newsletter

HOWUL
A LIFE'S JOURNEY
DAVID SHANNON

"Un-put-down-able! A classic hero's journey, deftly handled. I was surprised by every twist and turn, the plotting was superb, and the engagement of all the senses – I could smell those flowers and herbs. A tour de force"

– LINDSAY NICHOLSON MBE

Books are dangerous

People in Blanow think that books are dangerous: they fill your head with drivel, make poor firewood and cannot be eaten (even in an emergency).

This book is about Howul. He sees things differently: fires are dangerous; people are dangerous; books are just books.

Howul secretly writes down what goes on around him in Blanow. How its people treat foreigners, treat his daughter, treat him. None of it is pretty. Worse still, everything here keeps trying to kill him: rats, snakes, diseases, roof slates, the weather, the sea. That he survives must mean something. He wants to find out what. By trying to do this, he gets himself thrown out of Blanow… and so his journey begins.

Like all gripping stories, *HOWUL* is about the bad things people do to each other and what to do if they happen to you. Some people use sticks to stay safe. Some use guns. Words are the weapons that Howul uses most. He makes them sharp. He makes them hurt.

Of course books are dangerous.

ISBN: 9781911409908 (epub, kindle) / 9781911409809 (200pp paperback)

Visit bit.ly/HOWUL

About Ben Gribbin

Ben Gribbin first fell in love with the sea when he was born in Brighton in 1976. Fascinated by fantasy and still in love with the sea, he uses these as major themes in his writing, particularly his poetry. He took his love for the sea with him when he studied at Trinity College, Dublin, for an MPhil in Creative Writing and Publishing, and spent any time not writing, or drinking Guinness, gazing wistfully at the beautiful Eastern Irish Coast.

Whilst living in London and pursuing a career in helping other people to publish their writing at a major publishing house, Ben wrote the first draft of his novel *Thomas Silent*. Several rewrites, 4 house moves, one wedding and 3 children later, Ben was excited to see *Thomas Silent* published by Elsewhen Press in 2015.

He also had *The Sad Happy Tale of Aberystwyth the Bat*, a novella for children, published in 2015. Ben has had poetry published in *Magma*, and *The Irish Poetry Review*.

He continues to love writing and the sea, working in his small box room in rural East Sussex, where he lives with his wife and children.